WAR IN WHITE CHOCOLATE

More books by Suzan Harden

(Each series is in suggested reading order)

Bloodlines

Blood Magick

Zombie Love

Zombie Confidential

Zombie Wedding

Amish, Vamps & Thieves

Blood Sacrifice

Love, War & a Bulldog

Zombie Goddess

Ravaged

Sacrificed

Reality Bites

Ghouls in the Grocery Store

Resurrected

Bloodlines Shorts Anthology

Bloodlines: The First Boxed Set

Seasons of Magick

Spring

Summer

Autumn

Winter

The Seasons of Magick Anthology

Justice

Sword and Sorceress 28 ("Justice")

Sword and Sorceress 30 ("Diplomacy in the Dark")

Justice: The Beginning

A Question of Balance

A Modicum of Truth

A Matter of Death

A Touch of Mother

A Twist of Love

A Virtue of Child

A Hand of Father

A Measure of Knowledge

A Hint of Thief

The Justice Thalia Stories

Snowfall

Murder Most Fowl

The Sweetest Poison

A Granddaughter of Mine

Tales of the Twelve
The Trickster Priestess and the Demon

Crossover Worlds
Invasion!

888-555-HERO
Hero De Facto
Hero Ad Hoc
Hero De Novo
A Very Hero Christmas
Hero De Jure
Hero In Camera
Hero Amicus Curiae
A Very Hero Wedding
Hero Ad Litem
Queer Eye for the Super Guy

Solar System Services, Inc.
Alone Is Not Lonely

Millersburg Magick Mysteries
Spells and Sleuths
Fae and Felonies
Magick and Murder

Soccer Moms of the Apocalypse
Pestilence in Pumpkin Spice
Famine In French Vanilla
War in White Chocolate
Death in Double Mocha

Miscellaneous
Sword and Sorceress 31 ("Pig-Headed")
Sword and Sorceress 32 ("Unexpected")
Practical Witches
Revenge Served Hot
The Yule Switch
Chocolate for Dinner
Silver Shoes and Pigs' Ears

For updates, news, and giveaways, join Suzan's mailing list or visit her website at www.suzanharden.com. You can also check her out on Twitter @Suzan_Harden or Facebook @SuzanHardenWriter.

WAR IN WHITE CHOCOLATE
(Soccer Moms of the Apocalypse #3)

ISBN-13 - 978-1-64918-018-6

Published by Angry Sheep Publishing
Findlay, Ohio

Interior Design by JW Manus
Cover Design by For the Muse Designs

War in White Chocolate

SUZAN HARDEN

Chapter 1

On Sunday evening, Wila Ardale sat in the lotus position on the thick, plush carpet of her family room with her eyes closed. Despite the nag champa incense wafting through the air and her yoga pose, she jerked when pots banged in her kitchen. Her role as War, the third Horseman of the Apocalypse, or rather Soccer Mom of the Apocalypse as her friends preferred to call themselves, seemed to feed on her PTSD. The same PTSD she believed she had mostly dealt with after she left the army nearly fifteen years ago.

Her right eye opened and peered up at Grandpapa's antique clock on the stone mantel above the fireplace. Five frickin' minutes. It had been five frickin' minutes and she couldn't even get into the first level of a meditative trance. Not with her grandmother rattling around in the kitchen.

Her recently risen from the dead Gammy.

Wila knew Gammy had dealt with her own stress by cooking when she was alive. Apparently, it held true in her resurrection. But the damn noise was driving Wila crazy. She was used to total silence on her days off work while Derek was at school or at his father's house like right now.

And the ex-louse would be bringing her son home at any moment. She trusted Derek to remain silent about Gammy living with them, and the ex-louse went out of his way to avoid talking to Wila. He would drop Derek off at the door as usual, and she wouldn't have the faintest chance of dealing with him for two whole weeks. So, why was she worried about Deion finding out about Gammy?

"Me-arow," Malcolm complained at another bang. Wila looked over at the couch. Her seal-point Siamese sat on his haunches on the middle cush-ion, cocked his head, and repeated his complaint. His blue-point brother Martin lay on the back of the couch and swished his tail in agreement.

"I know, I know," Wila muttered. "I'll go talk to her."

Martin sniffed to indicate he didn't think anything Wila said to Gam-my would work. With another round of banging from the kitchen, he had a point.

Wila stretched out for a count of fifteen before she rolled to her feet and padded into the kitchen. Gammy crouched before the open pots and pans cupboard, shuffling things around loudly.

"Whatcha looking for, Gammy?" Wila asked.

"Don't you have a colander, baby girl?" Gammy straightened.

Wila walked around the breakfast bar. A large bundle of collard greens sat in the sink. Yep, her grandmother was cooking again.

"Gammy, I told you that you don't have to cook every meal for us," Wila said. "And especially not tonight. Derek is eating dinner with—" It took all her will not to refer to Deion as the ex-louse in front of her grand-mother. "—his dad tonight."

Gammy shook her head sadly. "I can't believe you and Deion are di-vorced. I remember you two being so happy the day your blessed little baby was born."

"Well, that was before I found out he was screwing my best friend Rashida, our babysitter Kristy, and his secretary Eileen," Wila grumbled.

"Eileen?" Gammy's forehead wrinkled. "She's your mama's age, and she's white."

Wila crossed her arms and leaned her left hip against the counter. "Tell me something I don't know."

"Still need a colander for the greens." Gammy waved at the leafy vege-tables in the sink.

"I can throw a frozen pizza in the oven for dinner." Wila stalked over to her refrigerator. "That's plenty for the two of us."

"That processed food isn't good for you," Gammy lectured.

Wila took a deep breath before she turned to face her grandmother. "I can pick up soup, salad, and sandwiches from the café down the street. That would be healthier, right?"

Gammy shook her finger at Wila. "It's a waste of money eating out all the time. How are you going to save up for Derek's education by spending willy-nilly?"

"The money for Derek's education is already set aside." That had been the one thing she refused to compromise on during the divorce negotiations. Fortunately, the ex-louse didn't want to ruin his reputation in front of the family court judge.

"Fine, but that doesn't take care of these collard greens, baby girl. And I bought a nice ham hock, too."

Wila tensed at the reminder her friend Francine was doing more for Gammy than she was. Like buying Gammy clothes and taking her grocery shopping while Wila was at work. She didn't need a white savior to take care of her own damn family.

Guilt niggled at her. That wasn't fair to Francine. She made the same efforts for Wila as she did for Penny and Dani. It's just that Francine had blossomed as a Soccer Mom while Wila . . .

She was barely keeping her shit together.

Swallowing the raging anxiety, Wila pointed out, "I have a strainer I use for pasta."

"Too small." Of course, the old woman wanted a bigger colander. She was used to cooking for her eight children, their significant others, her grandchildren, and all the cousins. However, Mom and most of the aunts and uncles had passed. Dad lived in Florida with his girlfriend. And all the cousins had scattered across the fifty states to wherever their jobs took them. Just another reminder of how alone she was, except for Derek.

And Gammy.

"How about we go shopping in the morning?" Wila said. "We'll find you a colander you like, and I'll help you with cleaning greens before I head into work. Then I'll be out of your hair and you can cook to your heart's desire."

Gammy stared into Wila's eyes before she rested a warm, callused palm against Wila's cheek. "You always were a good girl, Wila."

Her eyes burned, and she laid her own hand over Gammy's. "You have no idea how much I've missed you."

Gammy laughed. "I admit I never thought the sounding of the trumpets on Judgement Day was going to be like this."

"Those sounding trumpets are what we're trying to avoid, Gammy," Wila said sternly. Because she couldn't think of failure. Not stopping the Apocalypse meant her son would never have the life he deserved.

The security system beeped, and Derek shouted, "Mom, I'm home!"

Speak of the devil.

"In the kitchen!" she responded.

He raced in, skidding on the hardwood, and hissed, "Dad's here."

His warning was too late to rush Gammy upstairs to her bedroom. Sure enough, the ex-louse walked in behind Derek. His confident swagger had first attracted Wila to him, but now, it just pissed her off.

She crossed her arms. "What do you want, Deion? None of your girlfriends are here."

"Ah, Wila, always a pleasure to speak with you." His equally confident smile faltered when he noticed who was standing beside her. "Gammy Latricia? B-but you're dead!"

"You got no right to address me with any familiarity, Deion Jackson." Gammy shook her index finger at him. "If my great-grandson weren't standing right here, I'd be giving you a piece of my mind."

"What is she doing here?" Deion spluttered.

Wila glared at him. "It's been three weeks since the dead started rising from their graves. You may not have a lick of compassion, but I'm not about to turn my grandmother away from my home."

Something alien shone from Deion's eyes, but this was normal human malice. He wasn't possessed by a demon, as much as she wanted to blame her ex's attitude on someone, or something, else.

"Derek, get in my car," he demanded.

Malcolm hissed at Wila's elbow. He knew he wasn't supposed to be on the counter, but she was rather amused that her cats disliked the ex-louse as much as she did. Maybe animals' instinctive distrust of her ex was the real reason he never wanted pets while they were married.

"What? No!" Derek protested. "I'll see you Wednesday after school. Like always."

Martin stalked into the kitchen and planted himself in front of Derek. The tip of the Siamese's tail twitched, a sure sign he was there to back up his brother.

"You had your weekend with our son, Deion," Wila said. "You've delivered him safely home. It's time for you to go."

Deion said nothing. None of his usual attempts to intimidate her or threaten her with legal action. Nor did he reprimand Derek for giving him lip. No, Deion pivoted and stalked out of her kitchen. She followed to make sure he exited her house, both cats on her heels, and she watched him back out of her driveway.

His silence indicated he planned something. Something she wasn't going to like.

Too bad her flaming sword didn't work on living ex-husbands.

Chapter 2

After carpooling Derek and the other three Soccer Moms of the Apocalypse's kids to school, Wila went home and managed to get through her daily yoga session in the family room and into her meditation before Gammy woke up and came downstairs.

"Morning, baby girl," she said cheerfully.

Wila opened her eyes. "Morning, Gammy."

"You still going to help me with those greens?" With that tone, Gammy wasn't asking a question.

Of course I am, Gammy." Wila climbed to her feet. "Don't we need to get you a decent colander first?"

Her grandmother frowned. "Don't get smart with me, young lady."

"I wasn't." Wila hugged her grandmother and kissed her cheek before she crossed to the kitchen table. After sitting down on one of her intact chairs, she pulled on her athletic shoes. "I need to pick up a few things at Arrow, too."

"You're not going to wear those pants to the store, are you?" Gammy scowled at her.

"What's wrong with them?" Wila looked down at her yoga pants expecting to see a stain or a tear.

"First of all, it's November, and it's too dang cold." Gammy scowled.

"It's been in the sixties the last two days." In fact, the unusual warm snap had both the local Oakfield weather reporters as well as those in the Chicago metro area making jokes that the end of the world was near. As if the dead walking around weren't enough. "I don't need anything warmer."

"Well, they are too tight for you to be wearing them out in public," Gammy admonished. "I admit you're fine looking woman, but boys will think you're a female of loose morals."

Wila finished tying her shoes and stood. "Gammy, styles have changed a little bit since you were my age. And as for loose morals—" She concentrated and manifested her flaming sword. "If anybody thinks they can try anything with me, this will make them think differently."

"All right, but don't blame me if you get stared at for wearing tight pants while swinging a flaming sword," Gammy muttered.

"You didn't mind Errol Flynn in tight pants and brandishing a sword in those old black and white movies," Wila teased.

"That's different," Gammy mumbled, looking everywhere except at Wila.

She laughed as she grabbed her keys off the breakfast bar. "Get your jacket, and let's get that colander."

      🔥   💀   🔥

Wila offered to let Gammy push the shopping cart through the big-box department store.

Gammy waved a dismissive hand. "Don't need it for support anymore, baby girl. It's strange, but my joints aren't hurting me like they used to. The Lord has taken my pain away like He promised in the Good Book."

That was one of the small blessings of the risen dead. And it was fun watching her grandmother's amazement at some of the new tech that had come out in the last ten years.

"Now why on earth does anyone need just one cup of coffee?" Gammy said as she stared at the row of tiny coffee makers on the shelf in the kitchenware section. "I would have thought those things would have died out by now from all the waste."

"Derek doesn't drink coffee, and there's no sense in making an entire pot for me," Wila said. "Mine comes in handy."

"If you make a full pot, you'd have enough for both of us for the entire day," Gammy insisted.

"And it tastes like burnt sludge after it sits for that long," Wila protested. "I never knew how good coffee could taste until Penny opened Java's Palace."

Gammy snorted. "I can't believe your friend makes a living selling expensive, fancy coffee and breakfast foods the entire day."

Wila laughed. "You need to hang out with her father-in-law Edward. He agrees with you."

"I am not spending time with a married man," Gammy snapped.

"He's widowed—" Wila stopped herself. "Actually, I'm not sure what a person is if their dead spouse comes back to life."

"I already feel bad enough for Laura." Gammy said softly. "I don't know what I would have done if I found out your grandfather was keeping time with another woman."

"That's not really fair though." Wila sighed. "It took Edward two years to finally move on with his life, and he just started seeing Marian shortly before the Apocalypse started."

"I suppose that's true. Is Penny bringing Laura along to your girls' night on Wednesday?" Gammy asked with a hopeful tone.

"I'm sure she will." Wila chuckled. Her grandmother was old enough to be Laura's mother. But the two of them had bonded over their resurrected status.

"I wonder if Otis will show up at our old house in Chicago," Gammy murmured.

"Turk promised to call if Pappy does." Wila's cousin had bought Gammy's house on the South Side after Pappy died because she didn't have the money to maintain it. However, Wila was pretty sure Turk hadn't believed a word she said when she called him about Gammy's resurrection.

Wila and Gammy turned down the next aisle of housewares. Different utensils hung on the walls. Each grouped by designer color instead of function.

"Now, why does anyone need lime green spatulas, hot pink mixing bowls, and purple paring knives?" Gammy didn't wait for an answer to her rhetorical question. Instead, she glared at the labels for each utensil. "And these prices are just plum foolish!"

"I hate to tell you, but this is one of the cheapest stores these days."

Gammy picked up a spatula that matched the purple paring knife. "And these plastics are so thin. We had much sturdier Tupperware in my day."

"They're silicon, not plastic, and I thought we were looking for a large colander," Wila said wryly.

You watch your mouth, young lady." Gammy tried to look over the reading glasses that had been normally perched at the end of her nose when she was alive, but since she rose from the grave, her eyesight was twenty-twenty. Wila had even taken Gammy to the opthamologist who rented space in this store to make sure.

Gammy marched down to the end of the aisle where the stainless steel kitchen utensils shone under the store's fluorescent lights. She picked up a large colander and shook her head. Wila pushed the cart in the same direction.

"Can you believe this thing costs more than I made in a week cleaning houses when your mama was a little bit?" Gammy shoved the price tag in Wila's face.

"That's actually a good price." Wila flicked the metal with her forefinger. It pealed a bright note. "Decently made. Big enough for that mess of greens you bought."

"B-but . . ." Gammy poked her head around the corner. "This is it. All there is." Her shoulders slumped. "I can't let you spend your money on this. I'll make do—"

"Gammy." Wila laid a hand on her grandmother's shoulder. "It's okay. I can afford it."

"You've got a boy to raise, and now an extra mouth to feed, a-and—"

"Family looks out for each other," Wila said fiercely. "Isn't that what you always told me?"

"This wasn't—" Gammy's body trembled beneath Wila's touch. "This wasn't what I expected the afterlife to be like." Gammy reached up and patted Wila's hand.

"You expected bad coffee and cheap Tupperware in Heaven?" Wila teased.

Gammy laughed. "You are being evil, child."

"No, I want to make my grandmother happy." Wila gently pulled the stainless steel colander from Gammy's hand and set it in the shopping cart. "Now, let's get the rest of the things I need. Afterward, we'll stop for expensive coffee and fancy sandwiches at Penny's café."

"Evil child." Gammy snickered. "Evil, evil child."

"With all due respect, that's evil woman," Wila shot back.

"What kind of evil things do you do?" a deep voice said behind her.

Wila whirled around to find a tall man with deep brown skin, equally deep brown eyes, and a high and tight cut. He was dressed in a medium gray suit accentuated by a scarlet silk tie. The man would be hot as hell if he didn't have an ugly ass demon crawling under his skin.

"Well?" he asked. "I'm curious about what evil things War would do."

Despite her heart hammering in her chest and the breath frozen in her lungs, Wila shifted so Gammy was behind her. She couldn't, wouldn't show her fear to this thing. "How about I simply kill you instead?" she forced out.

Except they were in a popular store, and it was getting busier by the moment. If she drew her sword, there would be too many questions. And the Soccer Moms already had enough trouble with reporters following Francine all over Oakfield after she was filmed turning into Famine during a confrontation with some vigilantes at one of the local cemeteries.

"What's wrong with his face?" Gammy whispered behind her.

"He's not a person. He's Satan spawn," Wila spat. She could barely keep her trembling in check as the panic attack grew, but the demon would take Gammy's soul if Wila gave in to the fear.

The demon placed a hand on its chest. "Well, now, that hurts my feelings, War."

Wila glared at it. "You don't have feelings."

It shrugged. "Well, that's true."

"Why are you harassing us?"

"Technically, I'm not harassing anyone." It grinned. "Is that one of the evil things you like? To be harassed by a hot package like the lawyer I'm riding?" Its hand trailed down the length of the torso of the poor man it had possessed.

"Leave now, or—" Wila manifested her sword. "—else."

"I love a woman who likes penetration." It sighed dramatically. "But not today, my dear, I have my own business with you and your sisters."

She frowned. It had to be lying. All demons lied. And they usually lied by telling the truth. Would Penny's husband Gene prescribe her something to keep the illogical thoughts from driving her crazy? She'd been off the antidepressants since she found out she was pregnant with Derek, and she'd been doing okay without them for the last thirteen years, thanks to her yoga and meditation.

"Aren't you even going to ask?" The demon seemed offended.

"I'm not stupid enough to bargain with a demon," she said. "I rather like my soul, and I plan on keeping it."

He smiled. "What if I offered my assistance to the Horsemen to stop the Apocalypse for something other than your souls?"

Chapter 3

Wila squelched the threatening hysterical laughter. "Now, why on earth would I believe that?"

"You haven't even heard my offer yet," it said with mock disappointment.

"I don't need to hear it to know it's utter bullcrap."

It clicked its tongue against its teeth. "Such an angry Black woman. Positively a textbook stereotype."

"I'm not an angry Black woman," she shot back. "I'm an irritated Soccer Mom with a flaming sword. And I've got a hankering for demon shish kebab." She lunged for the demon.

It danced out of reach of her steel. "Talk to your sisters, War. Before you all make a decision you'll regret. I'll be in touch." It backed out of the housewares aisle and disappeared around the endcap.

Wila started to follow, but Gammy grabbed her right arm. "Don't be a fool, child. He's taunting you to get you to act stupid. While I'd do my best to watch your back, I'm not your sisters."

"I don't have any sisters," Wila growled.

"Penny, Francine, and Dani may not be your kin by blood, but the four of you are tighter than any family."

Gammy was right about the demon as much as it burned Wila to admit it. The bastard could have an associate waiting for her to leave Gammy alone. It wouldn't be the first time the demons kidnapped a family member of the Soccer Moms to use as a hostage against them. As one of the resurrected, Gammy was super vulnerable. Only God knew was else the demons could do with a human soul.

Besides use them to kill the Soccer Moms of the Apocalypse.

And Gammy was right about the other Soccer Moms, too. They'd always been there when Wila needed someone. Even Francine, who normally irritated the hell out of Wila.

Wila closed her eyes and evened out her breathing. The weight of the steel in her hand faded. When she felt calm enough, she opened her eyes.

"Let's pay for your colander, and get out of here," she muttered.

"What about your own shopping list?" Gammy protested.

"Those things can wait." Wila softened her voice. She didn't need to take her bad mood over the demon out on her grandmother. "Right now, I need coffee and a talk with one of my so-called sisters."

The parking lot in Java's Palace was more than half full when Wila turned into it twenty minutes later. She and Gammy wasted fifteen of those minutes in the check-out line when Arrow's store computer crashed and all the registers went down. If Wila were a betting woman, she'd lay a week's paycheck the damn demon who'd confronted her was behind the computer issues.

She parked her red minivan next to Penny's white one. It would give Scarlett and Silver a chance to spend time together. Wila couldn't say how she knew it, but the four Soccer Moms' minivans/horses seemed to communicate with each other, especially about their drivers/riders. It was freaky as hell, but it was just one more element in the weirdness her life had become.

They entered the coffee shop. Penny's assistant manager Josie grinned at them from beneath her mop of wild pink curls as they approached the counter.

"What can I make for you this morning, Wila?"

"My usual, Bubblegum, but I also need to talk to Penny. I thought she worked today."

"She's in the back doing inventory." Josie reached for a large paper coffee cup and scribbled their code for a white chocolate mocha and handed it to Oliver who was manning the espresso machines.

"Gammy, order whatever you want. I'll be right back." Wila handed her grandmother her debit card and strode down the hallway toward the café's store room. She opened the door. The light was on. "Hey, Penny!"

"I'm in the back!"

Wila followed Penny's voice to the corner of the store room. "We've got a problem."

"Besides my missing shipment of large cups?" Penny rose from where she crouched and counted plastic-wrapped stacks of coffee cups on a shelf. She set aside her clipboard and pen before she brushed an auburn lock that had escaped her ponytail behind her ear and grinned.

"More like demon trouble."

Penny's smile fell, and she swore under her breath. "Another team try to kill you and/or kidnap your grandmother?"

"Actually, this was a new tactic." Wila hugged herself. Things could have gone very badly at the super store. "A demon approached me while Gammy and I were picking up some things at Arrow. He made some nasty comments, but nothing worse than the shit our dear Officer Pence has said to me." The beat cop had it out for all the Soccer Moms because they failed to stop a demon from killing his own resurrected grandmother.

Well, lying to him the night Penny's daughter Justine was kidnapped by demons and the entire staff of Penny's coffee shop were possessed didn't exactly help the Soccer Moms' reputation as far as Pence was concerned.

Wila frowned as she replayed this morning's incident in her head. "The demon said it would help the Soccer Moms stop the Apocalypse for something other than our souls, but it didn't specify what. It also said I needed to relay the offer to my sisters, and it would be in touch. And the weirdest part was that it just walked away. Not one move to hurt me or Gammy, much less any threats."

Penny's right eyebrow rose. "Do you believe it?"

"It's a different play than interfering in our lives or trying to kill us out-right." Wila shrugged. "But no, I don't believe it. I can't figure out why a demon would want to stop the Apocalypse."

It was Penny's turn to shrug. "Maybe they're worried their boss will lose the war, and they won't have humans as playthings anymore. Or one of the translations I read they'd be condemned to non-existence once the Lamb and His armies won."

"Maybe." Wila shook her head. "There's something else. Gammy could see it was a demon."

"Really?" Penny's eyes widened. "My mother-in-law was trained on what to look for, but your grandmother?"

"I know. She caught me off guard, too."

"If any of the other dead can see demons through a possession . . ." Penny's attention was lost in her analysis of the situation from every conceivable angle.

"Has Francine or Dani mentioned anything about the dead being able to see demons?" Wila prompted.

"Neither of them has said anything to me," Penny said. "Should we call them?"

"No. I'll text a warning to them in case this idiot shows up again." Wila sighed. "We can discuss it in depth during our girls' night. Is Laura coming with you?"

"Yeah." Penny grinned. "She likes your grandmother."

"And the situation with Edward and Marian is still driving her crazy." Wila laughed.

"She's honestly trying to remind herself their vows were until death do us part." Penny leaned closer to Wila. "Would you believe Gene told Edward if he didn't like Laura staying with us, he could move in with Marian?"

"And what did Laura and Marian say to that?"

"Marian refuses to sleep with him, much less have him stay at her con-do. She's of the opinion Laura's resurrection nullifies her death. Therefore,

Edward and Laura are still technically married." Penny sighed. "On the other hand, Laura says her death ended their marriage, she has the right to date, and Edward can—and I quote—go screw Deborah Gibson's brains out—as far as Laura is concerned."

Wila cocked her head. "Who the hell is Deborah Gibson?"

"A neighbor Edward was having an affair with while Laura was in hospice."

"What!" Wila stared at Penny. "Mr. I'm So Conservative I Make the Amish Look Like Punk Rockers had an affair?"

"I'm afraid so." Penny grimaced.

"I know damn well he wouldn't admit that to Gene, much less you. And I thought Laura didn't remember the last year or so of her life."

Penny sighed. "She doesn't. Deborah recognized Laura when we were at the grocery store over the weekend, and with the coming Apocalypse, she decided she needed to beg for Laura's forgiveness for committing adultery with Edward."

"Oh, my god. What did Laura do?"

"She cold-cocked the bitch."

Wila pursed her lips in an attempt not to laugh.

Penny chuckled. "Go ahead and laugh. I did when it happened."

Wila roared at the thought of some elderly woman thinking a badass demon hunter like Laura Hudson wouldn't slap her silly for screwing with Laura's husband.

When Wila finally got her mirth under control, she said, "This Gibson woman isn't going to sue Laura, is she?"

Penny shrugged. "If she does, how's the court going to handle it? Laura may be running around now, but legally, she's dead."

"Is that what you think, or is that what Fred Whittaker said?"

"It's the opinion of the attorney Fred referred me to," Penny amended.

A chill ran through Wila. The demon she and Gammy encountered at Arrow claimed to be riding a lawyer, but the timing couldn't be a coincidence. She pulled out her phone. "What's the name of the guy you talked to?"

"Chance Paxton."

Wila tapped the name into her phone. A local listing came up with a picture. Her heart stopped. She turned the phone to Penny. "This the guy?"

"Yeah." Penny looked up at Wila, and her face turned sheet white. "No. Oh, no."

"Yep. This was the demon who confronted me at Arrow."

Wila wanted to scream. The shit that went down with Seth Rimmon had been bad enough. Through Chance Paxton and his legal contacts, this demon could make their lives living hell.

Chapter 4

"Let's go to this guy's office, and kill this demon's ass," Wila snarled.

"No." Penny's hand sliced through the air. "In the immortal words of Admiral Ackbar, it's a trap."

"So, what exactly is this demon up to?"

"Like you just said, they're trying a new tactic." Penny frowned as she looked at the picture on Wila's phone screen again.

"If I wasn't scheduled to work this afternoon, I'd say let's have our girl's night tonight," Wila grumbled.

"Heck, I should keep a bottle of premade margaritas in my desk." Penny smiled. "I have the blenders and ice here. Unfortunately, the soccer coaches rather insist on sticking to the practice and game schedule."

Wila rubbed the achy spot between her eyebrows. "You know the demon may have given you the wrong information about Laura's situation."

"I got a second opinion from your divorce attorney," Penny said. "She said the same thing, and I met with her in person. I may have talked to the real Paxton on the phone last Thursday."

Wila dropped her hand. "How is Lilah?"

"She's fine. I forgot how feisty she is for someone older than my mother-in-law." Penny chuckled.

"Speaking of old ladies, I left Gammy out in the dining room."

Penny picked up her clipboard and pen. "I'm due for a break anyway. Is it okay if I join you?"

"Gammy would love it."

Wila strode out to the hallway and headed for the dining room. As she passed the counter, Josie called out her name.

"Yes?" She paused.

"Give me a sec to steam the milk for your coffee." Josie shifted to the closest espresso machine. "I wasn't sure how long you would be back with the boss, and I know you like your mocha extra hot."

Wila grinned as she approached the counter to collect her drink. "Bubblegum, I don't know what Penny would do without you."

"Penny would be mixing alcohol with her coffee and losing all her business," Penny said as she stepped behind the counter to brew her own concoction.

"Rum goes really well with the peanut butter latte," Josie volunteered.

Wila hid a snicker while Penny paused in squirting pumpkin spice syrup into her mug.

Josie's cheeks matched her hair, and she mumbled, "Just sayin'." Her focus on pouring the steamed milk into Wila's cup was more than was normally warranted.

"Don't give Bubblegum the evil eye, Penny," Wila chided. "You were a college student once upon a time."

"What's that supposed to mean?" Penny glared at her over the top of the espresso machine she used.

"It means you could get more creative with your alcohol than I could while stationed in Germany." Wila shook her head. "There's only so much beer a woman can drink before it totally ruins her palette."

"That's because beer sucks." Josie handed Wila her white chocolate mocha.

In turn, Wila raised her extra-large cup in a salute to the assistant manager. "Amen, sister."

Once Penny completed her pumpkin spice latte, they crossed to the dining area to where Gammy sat enjoying her sandwich—egg, bacon, and cheese on an English muffin. Wila slid into the booth beside Gammy while Penny sat on the opposite seat.

Gammy looked around before she whispered, "You told Penny about that demon in the department store, right?"

"Yes, ma'am, I most certainly did," Wila assured her grandmother.

"You girls need to take care of him before he hurts somebody." Gammy's attention shifted to Penny.

"We need to find out what he's up to first," Penny said.

"But with all the formerly dead hunters staying at the Catholic church, surely you have enough people to watch your backs while you kill this one." Gammy took another bite of her sandwich.

The Vatican had refused to send any more living demon hunters to Oakfield, despite Father Perez and Father McAvoy's entreaties, other than Karen Longstreet. But once the resurrected hunters found out about the need of the Four Horsemen of the Apocalypse, they poured into the city. Father McAvoy took charge of the risen hunters and assigned one to each of the Horsemen's family members when the Horseman wasn't available.

Some of the oldest hunters thought Wila and her friend's calling themselves the Soccer Moms of the Apocalypse was sacrilegious, but Sister Joan and several other nuns thought the moniker was totally appropriate.

"If the demons are trying a new tactic to get their hands on the risen, the last thing we want to do is put them in harm's way," Wila protested.

"We need to run this past Father McAvoy." Penny glanced at her watch. "I can't get out of here until Valerie gets here at one."

Out of an abundance of caution, the Soccer Moms visited the rectory at Saint Michael's Church in person when they needed to consult with the members of the taskforce. That way, they could confirm whether the person they spoke with was free from demon influence.

"Dani's at work, and Francine is with Karen and Sister Joan training the police on dealing with demons today," Wila said.

Penny chuckled. "I know. I'm picking up the kids from school today and taking them to soccer practice this afternoon."

Gammy patted Wila's arm. "Baby girl, drop me off at the house, then go over to Saint Mike's before you gotta be at work."

"I promised you I'd help with the greens." Wila stared at her grandmother. The old woman never let any of her grandchildren avoid work, much less break a promise."

"Your role as a Soccer Mom is far more important than washing and tearing a mess of collard greens," Gammy stated firmly before she turned to Penny. "Have you thought about staying open later in the evening?"

Leave it to Gammy to change the subject to prevent any more arguing.

"No," Wila said. "You're not hitting up my friend for a job."

Gammy shrugged. "Laura and I need something to do besides putter around our family's houses."

"I can take care of you," Wila protested.

"I know you can, baby girl." Gammy reached over and patted her hand. "But I've been taking care of myself all my life. I don't see why I can't contribute to your household while I'm living there."

"Besides, Wila, weren't you the one suggesting Java's Palace stay open twenty-four hours when you're on the late shift?" Penny's brown eyes twinkled as she took a sip of her coffee.

"We weren't in the middle of the Apocalypse when I said that," Wila shot back.

"It's not a bad idea though," Penny said. "I've been thinking about leasing a second space sooner rather than later. The owner of Waterford Crossing contacted my real estate broker last week about a storefront I checked out last month. He's willing to make a lot of concessions in order to rent out the space."

"Is this the corner spot where the Mongolian restaurant used to be?" Wila frowned.

"Yep."

"You said it needed a ton of work."

Penny nodded. "Still does. The owner's willing to do the clean-up and build out of the place, and he's willing to knock off twenty-five percent of the monthly rate for the first year."

Suspicion raced through Wila. "Why?"

Penny pursed her lips. "Oh, he wants to make sure he goes to Heaven."

"You can't promise him that!"

"Keep your voice down, baby girl," Gammy murmured.

Yep, everyone was staring at the loud Black woman. The world may be ending, but some things simply didn't change.

"I didn't promise him any such thing," Penny said. "Nor did he actually say that's what he wanted. But with Francine being outed on the news as Famine and everyone getting sick here at the cafe, more people are putting two and two together than just Mayor Oldham and Chief Wright. But I'd be a fool not to take a prime offer." She grinned. "Especially when we stop the Apocalypse."

If they stopped the Apocalypse, but Wila wasn't going to ruin Penny's good mood by saying it out loud. Besides, maybe getting Gammy out of the house a couple of days a week would brighten her outlook.

It would definitely help with Wila's meditation exercises if her grandmother wasn't banging pots and pans most of the day.

"All right." Wila held up her hands. "We need to find you a car then, Gammy."

"You're not buying me a car," her grandmother snapped.

"Damn straight, I'm not." Wila grinned. "It's a loan with payments and interest that you will pay back to me." It was the same lecture Gammy had given her in high school.

"Well, then." Gammy sniffed. "I guess I can agree to that."

"Great." Penny nodded. "You want to start training Wednesday morning?"

"Yes, ma'am." Gammy practically jiggled on the bench.

Wila glared at Penny. "You're only saying that because you know I have the day off Wednesday, and the ex-louse is picking Derek up from school."

"Ex-louse?" Gammy narrowed her eyes.

"And you'll have the time to talk to Neal about getting something for your grandmother to drive." Penny sipped her coffee before she added, "If Gammy Wilkinson is willing to drive Laura to and from Java's Palace, I'll chip in half the car payment."

Wila groaned. "Why do I feel like I've been set up?"

"We're just being practical." Gammy patted her hand again.

Except their practicality made Wila feel incompetent for not being able to take care of her own family.

Chapter 5

An hour later, Wila pulled into the parking lot of Saint Michael's Church. She didn't like leaving Gammy alone at the house before Sister Joan arrived, but she had to trust the sigils Penny's father-in-law Edward instructed her to paint over the doors and windows would keep any demons out of her home. It would explain why the demon waited until they entered the Arrow department store this morning before it confronted them.

But then, things had been changing so much in her life Wila hadn't had a chance to take stock of it all. Such as the weird mix of older vehicles and rentals constantly parked at Saint Mike's without an event scheduled. She pulled into the spot next to Father Perez's tiny red hatchback. Since the demon hunters started pouring into Oakfield, a group of the parishioners had posted parking signs along the row closest to the church buildings. However, the signs were humorous labels for the people living and working at the little Catholic complex over the last month.

Most of the signs literally read "Demon Hunter". Then there was "Kick-Ass Nun", "Current Priest", "OG Priest", and "Mary, Wife of Jesus". But the best were the four marked with "Soccer Mom".

Wila pushed the button to turn off her vehicle, but her minivan/horse rumbled her displeasure via her engine.

"Baby, I told you before—" Wila stroked Scarlett's steering wheel. "—if they put up a sign saying 'Horse', some idiot will leave their animal here. You're so much better than a regular horse. Do you want some idiot animal taking a dump in your spot?"

A puff of steam floated from under the hood, and the engine stopped. Apparently, Wila's crass point mollified Scarlett. For now anyway, but her horse would raise the issue again the next time they came to the church. Scarlett thought the Soccer Mom signs should be replaced with hers and her sister mares' names along with their designated rider.

Wila slid out of the driver's seat. She didn't bother to lock the minivan anymore. If some dirtbag was stupid enough to try to jack her ride, Scarlett would deliver said dirtbag to the police.

Again.

And that was assuming said dirtbag could get past the patrols of the demon hunters and recruits guarding Saint Mike's. Speaking of which, Lucas Manewell and Brother Giuseppe approached her.

"*Buongiorno, Signora Guerra.*" The former demon hunting monk bowed. For someone born in Italy during the Renaissance, he was adapting damn well to twenty-first century life in America.

"Is there something wrong, m'lady?" Lucas frowned. He'd been one of the vigilantes Francine ran into at the Oakfield Cemetery the day the dead started rising. She had been forced to reveal her Soccer Mom persona of Famine to keep the idiots from shooting the newly resurrected folks. Unfortunately, that was when she was filmed as both human and Soccer Mom, and the video ended up on the news later that night.

Lucas had recognized what Francine was, and it spurred him to volunteer his assistance at Saint Mike's. The demon hunters took him under their wings, and in turn, Lucas had recruited his vigilante friends to be trained by the demon hunters. Subsequently, the former vigilantes assisted the local law enforcement and the Vatican demon hunters with protecting the public places where the resurrected were staying, like the other places of worship and the high school.

"No emergency yet, guys." Wila grinned. "This is a fact-finding mission."

Both men nodded and continued on their patrol. Lucas didn't presume he could answer her questions, and Brother Giuseppe didn't know enough

American English to answer though he probably had the knowledge. A misunderstood fact about demons due to a bad translation could be disastrous.

Out of manners, Wila entered the church itself to let Maria Cordero, the church's administrative assistant, know of her presence at the facility. Her husband's name was the reason for the signage for Maria's parking space. Jesus coached Derek's soccer team, the Tiger Sharks.

It didn't help that Derek had been making cracks about Coach Cordero being the Second Coming. However, that idea was a step too far for Wila to deal with right now. If it weren't for the dead starting to rise from their graves three weeks ago, she and the rest of her sisters would be in matching straightjackets.

Gammy was right. She was tighter with Penny, Dani, and even Francine than she had been with her brother Watende.

Wila popped the memory back in its little box with the rest of her past. It hurt too much to think about his and Mom's deaths. The irritating shrink the VA had set her up with said the trauma of the loss of her immediate family was twined with what she went through in Afghanistan. Maybe she needed to get a referral from Penny's husband Gene. The stress of being a Soccer Mom of the Apocalypse may be the proverbial straw that finally broke her.

She knocked on Maria's open office door.

Maria stopped typing and looked up from her monitor screen. "Hey, Wila!" A frown immediately marred her pretty face. "Sorry, I didn't hear the motion detector go off."

That may have been Wila's fault. Yet another new ability popping up with no clue of what she did or how to control it. But that wasn't any reason to scare the crap out of poor Maria.

Wila smiled. "It looked like you were pretty intent on whatever you were doing. Are Fathers Perez and McAvoy here? I had a weird experience with a demon this morning, and Penny sent me over to run it by them."

Maria's shoulders sagged. "Another one? Those things are worse than cockroaches."

"It's been a week since the last nest was cleaned out," Wila said. "One was bound to pop out of the woodwork sooner or later."

Maria picked up the receiver and pressed a button on her phone set. "Father? Wila's here with some questions." After a slight pause, she added, "She says she had a weird experience with a demon." Another pause. "All right, Father."

She hung up the receiver. "Father Perez will be here in a moment. He hopes you don't mind a walk back to the rectory. Father McAvoy injured himself on Saturday."

"Let me guess." Wila grinned. "The O.G. tried to keep up with his old team?"

Maria chuckled. "He may have been the youngest member at one time, but Fathers Mbaye and Lambert as well as Laura Hudson have died and been resurrected. Father McAvoy sprained his knee, and the only reason he's staying off of it is because Sister Joan threatened to tie him to his bed."

"You really shouldn't be gossiping, Maria."

Wila turned at the familiar masculine voice behind her. It was damn shame Father Perez was a priest. He was hot and kind. Things Dani needed in abundance. The girl hadn't even dated since her husband Heath died in a car accident six years ago. Heck, she even refused when Wila offered to set her up with Ramon, a fellow paramedic who was attracted to Dani.

"It's not gossip when the Soccer Moms need to know who's available in a fight, Father," Wila said. "Not to mention, he is the senior living Vatican taskforce member here. We need his brains and his English skills right now. What I don't need is McAvoy getting himself injured or killed trying to prove he can keep up."

She looked back at Maria. "Did he go to a doctor?"

The administrative assistant shook her head.

Wila faced the younger priest again. "Then as your resident EMT, I'm going to check out his knee while I tell you guys what happened this morning."

"Actually, I'd be grateful if you did," Father Perez said with a rueful expression. "He'd listen to you about seeing a doctor."

Wila rolled her eyes. "You men are all the same." She waved at Maria. "See you at the soccer game tomorrow night?"

Maria smiled. "I'll be there."

Wila strode down the back hallway of the church beside Father Perez. They'd have to pass through the community center to reach the rectory.

"How's the rehoming going?" she asked.

"All the parishioners who can have taken in the recently risen." He shook his head. "We still have dead folks trickling in though."

"Has the Vatican figured out the rhyme or reason for the order of the dead coming back?"

Again, the priest shook his head. "They've called in some of the top mathematicians in the world. It seems to be totally random. Can I ask why?"

Wila sighed. "Dani was stressed about her mom or her husband showing up on her doorstep at first. Now, she's feeling a little left out."

"As long as the dead continue rising, we don't have to worry about the Sixth Seal," he said.

"Do we know that for sure?"

"No," he said grimly. "I believe, but I never thought I'd see the end times."

"It ain't over yet, Padre." She grinned.

The community center wasn't as busy as it had been, but a glance at the gymnasium showed it was still about a third full. Francine had been turned into a liaison between Oakfield's city and county governments, the local religious institutions, and the regional Red Cross office. And she was damn good at it, too. She'd been getting a ton of kudos through the city while she helped manage the crisis.

Which was driving Courtney Lasser, the president of the Oakfield Parents Association, absolutely crazy.

Metal clashed in the kitchen, and a female voice called out orders with military precision as Wila and Father Perez passed by the entrance.

She glanced at the priest. "Should I ask who took over cooking duties?"

"Sister Flavia." He smiled. "She's a force to reckon with, but she's one heck of a chef."

"I can't believe how many women worked for the taskforce when they didn't have rights anywhere else in the world," Wila remarked.

"Is this going to be another rant about the Mother Church and its misogynistic tendencies?"

"Sorry, Father." She shot him an apologetic smile. "It's more a rant about men in general. My ex-husband freaked out last night about my dead grandmother living with me. Or rather, he's freaked she's in the same house as his son."

"Not everyone has welcomed the resurrected people back like you Soccer Moms have."

She shook her head as they passed the classrooms that had been turned into nurseries for the risen children. "It's one thing to see my Gammy again, but why would God force these children back to earth after they had such horrible deaths?"

"I wish I had an answer for you." Father Perez pulled open the door into the rectory.

"Deke!" someone shouted.

Wila exchanged looks with Father Perez before they took off at a run through the house. When they reached the sun room, demon hunters and priests gathered around someone lying on the floor.

"Paramedic! Move out of the way!" Wila shoved past the unhelpful observers to find the person on the floor was Father McAvoy. His friend Father Mbaye knelt next to him. McAvoy spoke, but his words made no sense.

The resurrected priest originally from Africa stared at her with a panicked expression. "He's possessed!"

Chapter 6

"He's not possessed!" Wila crouched on the other side of Father McAvoy. "What happened?"

"He was sitting on the chaise, icing his knee, and we were talking," Father Mbaye said. "He started slurring his words, and I teased him about stealing some of the sacramental wine. Then he slid off the lounge, and I couldn't understand a word he was saying. It was like he was speaking in tongues."

Drool oozed down the left corner of Father McAvoy's mouth. His right eye seemed to focus on her, but not the other eye. She took his right hand in hers.

"Father McAvoy, can you squeeze my hand?"

He did. For a seventy-something-year-old man, he had a surprisingly strong grip.

She looked up at the younger priest. "Father Perez, call 9-1-1. Tell the dispatcher there's an off-duty paramedic on site. Have them patch you through to the rig they dispatch, and place your phone on speaker." She glared at the others gathered around Father McAvoy. "The rest of you? Get out!"

Father Perez stepped away from the surge of hunters leaving the sunroom. Wila caught a glimpse of her reflection in a window. Sometimes, War's red eyes came in handy.

She inhaled deeply and released it before she looked at Father McAvoy again. "I'm going to check your pulse, and then I'll ask you a series of questions, Padre. Squeeze my hand once for yes. Twice for no. Got me?"

He squeezed once.

Wila placed her index and third fingers against his left carotid artery. She counted heartbeats against the ticking of the second hand of her watch and repeated the same evaluation with his breathing. Checking the right side of his neck was worrisome. No heartbeat at all.

"Are you feeling dizzy?"

One squeeze of his hand.

"Can you see out of your left eye?"

Two squeezes.

"Wila?" Father Perez crouched next to her. "The other paramedics are on the phone."

"Ardale? What's the situation?" Dick asked.

Relief filled her. The older man knew his stuff. She wasn't looking forward to his retirement.

Assuming she and her sisters found a way to stop the Apocalypse.

Wila rattled off Father McAvoy's vitals. "Strong pulse in the left carotid. None detectable in the right. No vision in the left eye."

"Keep running through the symptom checks," Dick said. "I'll call Oakfield's ER and let them knew they've got a possible stroke victim incoming. We're five minutes out."

"Roger that." Wila winced as the words slipped from her tongue. Dick and Ramon would be giving her a ton of shit for at least a month for slipping into military vernacular.

Father McAvoy squeezed her hand three times.

"Are you asking if you are having a stroke?"

One squeeze.

"Don't worry, Padre." She smiled at him. "Meds today can ensure a full recovery if the docs can get them in you soon enough. Luckily, this happened when you were surrounded by your friends, so we caught this in plenty of time. Do you understand?"

One squeeze.

"Good. Can I finish my questions so the ER docs know what's going on?"

One squeeze.

By the time Wila finished the stroke checklist, she heard the approaching siren of Dick and Ramon's rig. She was going to be late to work for the first time ever, but the Soccer Moms needed Father McAvoy more than she needed a job.

Apparently, word about Saint Mike's had spread through the station before Wila arrived for work. She got a round of applause from everyone when she strode into the station. Everyone except Captain Miller.

He shook his head and tugged on his belt. "You're late, Ardale."

She made a face. "Technically, I started my shift an hour early."

"In my office. Now." He turned and strode into his office without waiting for an answer.

Crap. What was going on? Her attendance record was perfect. Even with all the Soccer Moms stuff happening, she was always on time. She followed Captain Miller into his office and closed the door behind her. She didn't need the jackals to eavesdrop on this conversation.

The captain sat down and waved at the visitor chair. "Have a seat, Wila."

He never called her by her given name. He never called any of the paramedics by their given names.

She perched on the edge of the chair.

"Are you okay?" His rheumy eyes shone with concern. Between his silver hair and craggy features, he looked ten years older than Dick. In reality, he was ten years younger.

"I'm fine," she said uncertainly.

"Was Father McAvoy possessed?"

She blinked. "I beg your pardon?" He couldn't know who she was. The other Soccer Moms had bent over backwards to keep her identity secret after they'd been outed. During the demon attack on the resurrected at the high school three weeks ago, she'd worn goggles and a scarf to cover her face.

Captain Miller leaned back in his chair. "Dick put everything together after Francine Astin—"

"Coy-Astin," Wila automatically corrected.

"Coy-Astin," he repeated. "After she was caught on video. It hasn't gone beyond me and Dick, but to warn you, the identity of War has been a major topic of discussion at City Hall. I just want to know the truth if I need to cover for you. Was the priest possessed?"

Too many thoughts ran through her brain. However, Captain Miller had always done right by her despite the crap she got from a lot of other city personnel.

"No, the priest wasn't possessed," she said. "He's in his seventies, and he had a stroke. Now, tell me exactly what Dick said to you."

The captain ticked off the points on his fingers. "If Ms. Coy-Astin is Famine per the news video, then Penny at Java's Palace would be Pestilence since she was the only person in the building who didn't have an exotic disease. And all of you were at your house when Chuck Hernandez's daughter flatlined for no reason. She would be Death, right?" He smiled. "So logically, you would be War."

"Because of my military background?"

He chuckled. "If past or present jobs were the criteria, I think Penny would have been Famine, but I heard through the grapevine her daughter had cancer when she was in kindergarten."

"It was first grade." Wila twined her fingers together. Derek was so confused and scared when his friend Justine stopped coming to school. Deion told her to lie to her son, but she couldn't do that. If she'd only realized then how easily lying came to her former husband at the time, maybe she wouldn't have wasted another three years with him.

But she'd also been at Java's Palace when Pence and his former partner

Simmons had arrived shortly after the Soccer Moms had rescued Penny's staff from possession. Simmons wasn't stupid, but he hadn't said anything to Chief Wright about Wila. However, Pence . . .

Pence would keep silent in order to use the knowledge against Wila. Somehow. Someway.

"Wila, I'm not trying to poke my nose in your personal business." Captain Miller leaned forward and rested his forearms on his desk. "I just want you to know you have the backing of everyone in the department. If you need emergency time off, let me know as early as you can. I'll make sure your shifts are covered."

"Thank you" She blinked. "I think."

"And one last warning, Miles Pence has been reinstated."

She slumped in the captain's visitor chair. "Good grief. What's it going to take before the city does something about him?"

"The shrink the city called in cleared him for duty." Captain Miller shrugged. "Between the Eastwood brothers not remembering what happened at Pence's house, no evidence of trauma on Mrs. Pence's body, and what the other three Soccer Moms reported to the detectives on scene, Chief Wright doesn't have cause to dismiss him."

"You mean my ex did some fancy lawyer steps and got Internal Affairs to drop any potential charges against him."

A wry smile filled the captain's face. "His firm represents all the first responder unions in Oakfield. Including us."

"I know. It's just—" Well, damn. Now, she knew why Deion had waltzed into her house last night. What the hell had Pence told him?

Chapter 7

That question ran through Wila's head during the rest of her shift. Even her partner Brian Tucker commented on her silence when they stopped for dinner at Taco Man.

"Dime for your thoughts?" he said as they slid into a booth with their trays.

"A dime?" She cocked her head.

He shrugged. "Inflation. A penny's just not enough anymore."

She smiled at his lame attempt at a joke. Brian was such a dichotomy. Blond, blue-eyed, tall, model-handsome, yet shy, quiet, and a bookworm when he wasn't working out at the fire department's gym.

"If Captain Miller chewed you out for being ten minutes late because you were saving an old man's life—" Brian started.

"He didn't read me the riot act." She took a sip of her diet soda. What she really wanted right now was her favorite mocha from Java's Palace, but the café closed an hour ago. "He warned me the ex-louse managed to get Pence reinstated."

Brian shook his head as he poured hot sauce on his first taco. "That man is a menace to public safety."

"So's Pence."

Brian chuckled. "I wish I could say it was personal between the two of you, but he's a nasty piece of work to everyone."

"So's Pence."

"All right." Brian laid down his taco. "What did the ex-louse do this time?"

Wila blew a stray curl out of her eye. "He found out Gammy is staying with me and Derek. He tried to demand Derek return back to his house with him, but Derek refused."

"And the ex-louse threw his usual temper tantrum?" Brian picked up his taco and bit into it.

"No, that's the weird part." Wila frowned at the taco in her hand before she looked up at Brian again. "He went silent and left the house."

Concern filled Brian's face as he chewed and swallowed. "You want me to talk to Maggie?" As the county clerk, Brian's stepmother was up on all the legal gossip in Oakfield.

"Yeah." Wila pursed her lips. "If he's going to try to take Derek from me, I need to know."

"He's going to get custody of Derek based on what? Your grandmother coming back from the dead?" Brian scowled. "What's he going to do next? Sue the mayor for asking people to help house the risen dead?"

"Knowing him? Yes." Wila chuckled. "You know damn well he didn't offer a room or two in his mansion to house them."

"Doing so would displace his harem," Brian mocked. "You know we can't have that."

Wila slapped the table and laughed out loud. The humor didn't totally erase the weight on her shoulders, but it did ease the burden quite a bit.

The following evening, Wila pulled her rig into a parking spot labeled for emergency vehicles at the Oakfield Recreational Center. Thankfully, her partner had no problem scheduling their meal break during a portion of Derek's Tuesday night soccer games when they were on duty.

She slid out of the ambulance and snagged the Styrofoam cooler behind her seat. Brian grabbed the bags of burgers they'd picked up at Wilson's on the way to the soccer fields.

Helen Chow sat in the tiny shed at the gate, collecting the token fees from the spectators. A steaming cup with the Java's Palace logo sat on the inner counter. She grinned when Wila set the cooler on the outer counter. "Is that what I think it is?"

"Genuine soul food. Ham, collared greens, and black-eyed peas," Wila recited the contents. If they'd known homemade non-Chinese ethnic cuisine and chai tea bribes were all it took to get Helen on the Soccer Moms' side, they would have been doing this years ago.

Helen rubbed her hands together in glee. "So much better when it's from someone else's kitchen."

Wila handed Helen the money for hers and Brian's admittance. "Enjoy!"

"You never bring me any soul food," he said wistfully while they walked towards the bleachers.

"All of Gammy's recipes call for lard, and I can guarantee that is what she used in the pot she whipped up last night." Wila grinned up at him. "You sure you want that ruining your rock hard abs?"

He held up the bags of burgers. "And these don't?"

"Not when they're your crappy soybean burgers," she shot back.

"What if she substitutes vegetable oil for lard?"

"You expect to get a free meal from me when you insult my Gammy's cooking?"

"You have no palate, Ardale."

Her chuckle died when she spotted Pence. He and Rafe Estrada stood near the bleacher steps. She heard through the grapevine Pence's previous partner Simmons refused to ride with Pence anymore.

"Hey, Estrada," Brian said.

"Tucker." The police officer grinned. "I know why I'm stuck here. Whatcha doing at the park?"

Brian shrugged. "Dinner break so we thought we'd watch Ardale's kid play."

"Well, we can't play favorites, but I'll secretly cheer for the . . ." Rafe drawled.

"Tiger Sharks." Wila grinned.

Rafe winked and laughed while Pence stared icily at her.

Brian followed as she climbed to the top row where her friends sat. Whispers from the other parents followed, but none of them could look directly at Francine. Penny's mother-in-law Laura, Gammy, and Karen Longstreet, the one living demon hunter the Vatican deigned to allow them, sat on the bench below the Soccer Moms while Francine's ward Rose Dorchester sat next to her. The resurrected girl from the nineteenth century idolized both Francine's daughter Brittany and Penny's daughter Justine, and Rose had already begged Francine to let her play soccer in the spring.

"You're just in time for the second half kick-off," Dani said.

"What's the score?" Wila sat next to Dani.

"Tied at one-one."

Wila whistled. The Muskrats had been struggling the last five years, but the new kid from Somalia had cut through whatever mental block the team suffered from. Heck, the kid was better at training and encouraging his peers than Coach Riley was.

"Pence give you a hard time down there," Dani whispered.

Wila shook her head. "No, just shot me the evil eye."

"He didn't say anything to any of us." The corner of Dani's mouth quirked. "Probably he's mad we all saw him cry over his grandmother."

"Maybe." Wila was pretty sure in her and Dani's cases, there was more to Pence's attitude. He had said a lot of nasty things, but he was careful not to have witnesses. She shoved away any thoughts of Pence. Time to enjoy being a mom even if it was only for forty-five minutes.

"Your afternoon snack, Ms. Coy-Astin." Wila took the very full bag marked "C-A" and passed it down the row.

"Thank you," Francine said fervently. "What do I owe you?"

Wila waved away her offer. "It's on me for being Gammy and Derek's taxi service the last three weeks."

"Wait a minute! I'm tonight's kiddie carpooler, and I brought drinks," Penny protested.

"Which is why I brought everyone cheeseburgers, so quit your whining." Wila traded two wrapped burgers to Dani for her and Penny while Dani passed a white chocolate mocha and Brian's green tea from Penny to Wila.

"Hey, everyone!" Maria Cordero climbed up and sat next to Gammy. Ever since Penny saved Maria and Father Perez from a couple of possessed thugs at the beginning of October, the coach's wife made a point of sitting with their little group of outcasts during games.

"Everything okay at the church?" Wila asked.

Maria nodded. "After the initial scare. I dropped Father Mbaye off at the hospital to watch Father McAvoy."

The other three Soccer Moms stared at Wila. "Why is Father McAvoy in the hospital?" Penny ground out.

"First of all, he busted his knee on Sunday, trying to keep up with the resurrected folks," Wila said. "Then he had a stroke yesterday morning before I had a chance to talk to him."

"Don't worry," Karen added. "He's going to make a full recovery."

Francine swatted the back of the demon hunter's head. "You didn't tell me this? Is that what the meeting at the church was about last night?"

"Ow! Hey!" Karen turned to glare at Francine while she rubbed the spot at the top of her blue French braid. "You guys have enough to worry about. Father Perez made a command decision as the head of the parish."

"Tomorrow's my day off," Wila said to forestall any more hunter abuse. "I can give Father Mbaye a ride to the hospital and talk to both him and Father McAvoy. We can discuss the whole situation tomorrow at girl's night."

Her plan seemed to mollify everyone. The remaining burgers and coffees were doled out. Below on the field, the head referee set the ball on the line between the opposing forwards and blew his whistle to start the second half of the game. Brittany got the ball and made a sweet pass to Derek. Cheers from both team's families filled the air as the kids raced down the field.

Amusement ran through Wila at the sight of Courtney Lasser's son Kenny keeping well away from both Brittany and Justine on the green. Derek had said Kenny wanted to quit playing soccer after seeing Francine in full Famine mode while trick-or-treating, but Courtney wouldn't let him. On the other hand, Courtney had stopped going into Java's Palace and harassing Penny since Halloween. Between Justine decking Kenny on the field last month and Courtney slapping Penny, maybe both Lassers realized escalating the hostilities between them and the Hudsons wasn't worth the attorney fees.

None of the other parents sat near their group. If the members of the association hadn't been avoiding Wila and her sisters for years thanks to Courtney's bullying, their evasion of them might have been more noticeable after the stupid video showing Francine change into Famine aired on the news three weeks ago.

On the field, Derek and Tommy Hendricks passed the soccer ball back and forth, searching for an opening to feed it to Brittany or Justine. Tommy managed to get the ball to Justine, but the converging Muskrats cut her off from a clear shot. Justine crossed the ball in front of the goal with a high kick, and Derek headed it into the net.

Wila jumped to her feet and screamed louder than the other Tiger Sharks members and their parents. Or she did until Brittany Astin ran over and laid a kiss on Derek's cheek. Wila leaned over to look at Francine, who blushed furiously. Penny winced. Dani looked surprised.

"Is there something you ladies would like to tell me?"

"Not here, and not now." If anything, Francine's face practically glowed like a nuclear pile. "We'll discuss it tomorrow night."

"If there's something—" Wila started.

Gammy turned and glared up at her. "Baby girl, let it go for now. For your sake, and the sake of your relationships." She lowered her voice. "And get your eyes under control."

Crap. Wila closed her eyes and counted to ten in German.

And counted again to make sure.

She cracked her right eyelid open and peeked at Dani. "Safe?"

Dani nodded.

Wila expected Brian to say something. He had to have seen what had just happened. However, he remained silent.

She did her best to focus on the rest of the soccer match, but she couldn't stop thinking about Brittany kissing Derek. Okay, so it hadn't been on the lips. It could have been.

Did Derek know Brittany liked him? Did he like her in return? He hadn't shown any interest in girls. But he turned twelve in July, so it was only a matter of time before his hormones kicked into full gear. And girls matured faster than boys. Was Francine encouraging this behavior in her daughter?

The referees blew their whistles to end the game, and the two teams and their coaches lined up to high-five each other. Spectators started working their way out of the stands. From the gray clouds scudding across the sky and the chill breeze picking up, Oakfield's Indian summer was done.

Brian offered to assist Gammy down the steps of the aluminum stands, and she let him. Crap, now that Gammy had seen him, she'd start bugging Wila about dating him. But she wasn't stupid enough to let any company guy dip into her ink well, even if Brian was attracted to women.

Their group collected their preteens with congratulations all around for the three who had scored and Mark for a spectacular save as goalie that secured the Tiger Sharks win.

They exited the gate when Dani murmured in Wila's ear, "Demon."

Sure enough, the asshole she and Gammy had encountered at Arrow yesterday morning leaned against the passenger door of Wila's rig.

Chapter 8

"Francine, Karen, get everyone out of here," Wila said. "Brian, go with them."

"I'm not leaving you—" he started.

"That's an order," she snapped.

And prayed he listened to her. He didn't respond. She didn't dare turn around to look to see if he obeyed.

The demon grinned as Wila, flanked by Penny and Dani, approached her rig. "Thanks for getting rid of the wife and the dangerous Horseman. Or is Horsewoman these days? Horseperson?"

"What are you doing here?" Wila demanded.

"To make a deal with you and your sisters."

The shakes hit Wila. Hard. It had been so long since she experienced them. The sword popped into her hand without her even consciously summoning it.

"Wila?" Brian whispered.

She glanced over her shoulder. He still stood there, all six feet and five inches of him.

"Got your six," he said with a nasty scowl. He was an Afghan vet like she was. It was one of the reasons she loved him. But a demon was way out of his league.

"Brian, leave. Please."

"Ooo, Brian! You gotta tell me how you got the lovely lady to beg you," the demon mocked.

"We both know you're not Chance, so cut the bullshit," Brian growled.

"Oh, come on, Brian baby." The demon fluttered its eyelashes and took a fake demure pose. "You know I secretly had a crush on you, too."

"Stop taunting him." Wila brandished her sword at the demon. She didn't care who saw her. No one made fun of her friends.

The demon dodged to its left. "Penis envy much, War?"

Penny yanked Wila back and stepped between her and the demon. "Who are you, and what do you want?"

"You can call me Crucifer."

"Crucifer?" Penny laughed. "You mean liked cruciferous vegetables?"

"All right, Brussel Sprouts," Dani said. "You told Wila you wanted to make a deal. Out with it."

The demon straightened its tie. "It's nice to see Death can take my offer seriously."

"That's because I get everyone and everything in the end, sweetheart," she shot back.

"There is no deal. Cabbage here is lying," Wila said. "It's a demon. That's all they know how to do."

Coach Cordero and Maria stepped up to Penny's right. "It's been a long time, old friend," the coach said.

"Well, I'll be damned," Crucifer muttered as he stared in shock at the coach.

"You're already damned," Wila shot back.

The demon ignored her, his attention solely on Coach Cordero. "The prince and all of Hell has been looking for you for the last thirty-three years, and you've been in East Bumfuck, Illinois, this whole time?"

Jesus Cordero shrugged. "It's a nice town to settle in. Have a family. Put down some roots."

No. It couldn't be. Wila stared at her son's soccer coach. Derek had been joking. But *cordero* meant lamb in Spanish. It was the perfect camouflage. Hide in plain sight.

"Oh, *Dios mio*," Dani whispered.

"I'd rather deal with the big man, anyway." An ugly smile lay behind the face of the attorney Crucifer possessed. "Here's the deal. You have your bitches help me secure the throne of Hell, and I'll deliver the Morningstar. I'll even throw in the gift wrap for free."

"It doesn't work like that, Crucifer." The coach wore a sad smile. "I can't order them to do anything."

The demon snorted. "Really? You're going to play the free will card with me?"

"The free will card is always in play when it comes to humans." The coach glanced at Wila, Penny, and Dani. "Especially human women. Ask your prince if you don't believe me."

Crucifer looked at the Soccer Moms again. "Same deal, ladies."

"I thought we were bitches." Wila's shakes faded under the onslaught of cold rage. She'd been equally angry the night she found out about the ex-louse's affairs, and he'd called her that ugly name.

"Why do women always make things more difficult than they need to be?" Crucifer complained.

"Why have demons forgotten how to sweet talk *chicas*, Kale?" Dani twirled her scythe for emphasis. "Your boss did a better job with Eve."

"We're not going to—" Wila started before Penny elbowed her in the ribs.

Hard.

Penny stepped forward and cocked her head. "Give us forty-eight hours to consider your proposal."

"Good to see someone here has a lick of common sense." Crucifer pretended to tip a hat. "Thursday at seven. Say at your lovely café, Pestilence?"

"That's acceptable," she said coolly.

The demon walked over to a silver BMW and climbed inside before he tore out of the parking lot, tires squealing.

Wila breathed a sigh of relief and concentrated on the white bread lyrics of a Carpenters' song. The weight of steel in her hand faded, but her anxiety wasn't totally alleviated. Penny had just put the Soccer Moms and their families in mortal danger.

And that was something Wila couldn't let pass.

She grabbed Penny's arm and whirled her friend to face her. "Are you freakin' insane?"

"Stop," Penny hissed. She stared at Wila.

No, Penny stared at something behind Wila.

She slowly pivoted. Pence and Estrada eyed Wila's little group. The two cops stood next to several parents, a handful of kids, and a couple of referees, all watching the Soccer Moms. A little awe mixed with a lot of fear in the civilian faces. Estrada wasn't a bit surprised, but then Francine and Karen had been training law enforcement personnel on dealing with demons and possessed people.

Worst of all though, Courtney Lasser stood in front of the entire group, her phone raised and a taunting expression on her smug face.

"I knew there was something wrong with you witches!" she crowed. "And now I have proof!"

Chapter 9

A scream of rage threatened to erupt from Wila. Maybe Penny could turn the other cheek with that weasel, but she couldn't. "Give me that phone, you lying piece of—"

Brian grabbed her around her waist. "She isn't worth it, Wil."

"Ohmigod, Mom!" Kenny Lasser pointed at Wila. "Her eyes are red! She's a demon!"

"You wouldn't know a demon if it bit you in the ass, you little punk!" Wila tried to break free of Brian's hold, but she'd hurt her partner if she struggled any harder.

Coach Cordero stepped between the Soccer Moms and the crowd watching them. "It's time to go home, everyone. The game's over."

"I *knew* it wasn't just Francine Astin who was a freak of nature." Courtney practically danced on the concrete.

"Coy-Astin," Wila, Penny, and Dani said in unison.

"Whatever," Courtney said. "I'll make sure your faces are plastered over every newscast in the Chicago metro area, so everyone understands how unnatural you people are."

"Courtney, walk away now before you piss me off, and I lose control," Penny said.

"Or what," Courtney sneered.

"If I lose control, I could accidentally kill everyone here," Penny said. "Wila's sword can't harm humans. Dani can only take you when you've died. But me and Francine, we affect the living, and dying from starvation or the plague isn't pretty or pleasant. So, like the coach said. Leave now."

Wila stopped trying to break free from Brian at Penny's speech. The other spectators quickly and quietly crossed to their vehicles and left the park. Even Kenny seemed to have caught a clue and tried to drag his mother away from the Soccer Moms.

"Mom, please!" Tears ran down the boy's face. "Let's go home!"

Finally, Courtney relented but not without a murderous glare at Wila and her friends. Brian set Wila on her feet, but he kept a firm grip around her waist.

"Mrs. Lasser?" the coach called out.

"What?" she snapped.

"Remember the Golden Rule before you do anything you will regret," he said gently.

"I'll make sure you never coach in this state again!" She literally spit along with the words. "And I'll make sure no one hires your construction company. Ever!"

She and Kenny raced to her own minivan, climbed in, and peeled out of the parking lot.

Once all the spectators were gone except the two cops, a sneer crossed Pence's face. "You're lucky your partner held you back. I would have loved to arrest you for assault."

Estrada rolled his eyes. "And this kind of crap is why no one wants to ride with you." He elbowed Pence. "Let's go."

He followed Estrada to their patrol vehicle after a final glare at the remaining Soccer Moms.

Brian released Wila, but with Pence gone, her attention turned to the coach.

He shook his head and looked at Maria. "It never changes, does it?"

"What did you expect, honey?" She smiled up at him. "They're human."

Wila took a step closer to the people she'd known as the Corderos. She couldn't stop staring at them. "Derek was right, wasn't he?"

"Yes." The coach smiled at her.

"Francine's not going to believe this," Wila murmured.

Coach Cordero's smile widened. "Francine already knows."

Wila and Brian were called to the site of a two-vehicle accident on the freeway as soon as he radioed dispatch they were back on the clock. The work kept them occupied for a good couple of hours between keeping the driver of one of the cars calm and transporting his pregnant wife to the Oakfield Hospital ER.

On the way back to the station, Brian said, "Are we going to talk about this?"

She sighed. "Why aren't you scared?"

"Scared of what?"

"Of me. My friends. The end of the world."

He chuckled. "I hate to tell you this, but I've never been scared of you. However, I do appreciate you not ripping my arms out of their sockets when I tried to stop you from going after that Courtney woman."

"You didn't try to stop me," she muttered. "You did stop me."

"Now, who's lying to who here?"

Wila glanced at him. "You got me to stop and think. As much as I wanted to smack the shit out of Courtney Lasser, I didn't want to hurt you."

"Thank you for that." Brian remained silent for a couple of blocks. "For the record, I figured out what you and your friends were a month ago."

"How?" She glanced at him and turned back to the street in time for the traffic light ahead to change from yellow to red. She stepped a little too hard on the brake pedal. The seat belts kept both her and her partner from smashing their faces against the windshield.

"Sorry about that," she muttered.

"You want me to drive tonight?" he offered.

"No." She cleared her throat. "How did you know what we were before tonight?"

"Almost a month ago, I was on a blind date," Brian said.

"You went on a date and didn't tell me?"

Brian sighed. "He's a guy my aunt Ruthie set me up with. He bartends at her restaurant. We were parked, and—"

"Parked, or *parked*?" she teased.

"Now, you're being mean for the sake of being mean," he complained.

"Inquiring minds want to know." The light turned green, and she pressed the accelerator.

"Fine. We were making out."

"Did you use a condom?"

"Wila!"

"Hey, I'm a safety girl, just like Julia Roberts."

"Right . . ." he drawled. "We didn't get that far when Duane spotted four women on horseback. One of them was dressed in modern tactical gear, except the camo was red. And she looked an awful lot like that picture you showed me when we were first assigned together of you and your Humvee in Afghanistan. Duane freaked out and insisted I take him home. Three days later, the dead started rising from their graves."

"I'm sorry your date was ruined." And she meant it. It was hard enough being Black in a suburb like Oakfield. Being gay had to be just as bad for Brian. "You going to see this Duane again?"

"No. According to Aunt Ruthie, he packed his bags and went home to Wisconsin. He wanted to be with his family if the world was ending."

"What about you? Going to head back to Kokomo?"

"No. My family's right here. At the station and in this rig."

Her eyes burned at his words.

And they made her even more determined to stop the Apocalypse.

Chapter 10

On Wednesday morning, Wila pulled into the drop-off line at school.

"Bye, Mom! Bye, Gammy!" Derek was out of her minivan and racing towards the main doors before she could say a word. Part of her missed the loving little boy who would hug her goodbye, but if he was starting to be interested in girls, she needed to deal with being replaced in his affections.

"Thanks for the ride, Wila! See ya later, Gammy Wilkinson!" Mark exited her minivan at a little more sedate pace than her own son. Surprisingly, Mark hadn't said a word during the ride to school about Brittany kissing Derek yesterday. It wasn't like Mark to refrain from teasing Derek about something like that.

Oh, god, please don't let Chuck and Marty Hernandez give her son the same bad advice about women they gave Mark. She wouldn't be able to deal if Derek became a player like Dani's brother.

Or Derek's own father, the ex-louse.

Wila turned in the direction of Java's Palace to drop off Gammy. She still wasn't sure about her grandmother moonlighting at the coffee shop. Gammy had worked so hard her entire life. Why didn't she trust her own granddaughter to take care of her?

"Are you still fretting about the demon at the game?" Gammy asked.

"That's why the Soccer Moms are meeting with the priests this morning."

"Ah, so you're moping about Brittany kissing Derek," Gammy said with a satisfied tone.

"What?" Wila glanced up.

"Baby girl, he's growing up," Gammy murmured. "Are you going to give every girl who bats her lashes at him the evil eye?"

"I'm more upset Francine knew about this and didn't tell me," Wila grumbled.

"Things haven't changed that much since my day." Gammy sighed. "She's probably more terrified of Brittany growing up than you are about Derek."

"How would you know?"

"I have four of each. I know who gets stuck with the unintended babies."

"I think I'm more worried about Derek becoming a player like his father," Wila said softly.

"You don't have to worry about him. You raised a good boy, and he loves you."

Wila swallowed the lump in her throat as she turned into the Java's Palace parking lot. She pulled into a slot and turned off the ignition.

"Sister Joan and I will see you when you get home, baby girl." Gammy unbuckled her seatbelt and opened her door. She paused when Wila did the same. "Where do you think you're going?"

"I'm going in and getting some coffee like I do every Wednesday."

"You're going to be late to your meeting," Gammy said.

"Not as late as you're going to be for your new job if you don't get a move on." Wila grinned.

When they walked inside, Penny's senior assistant manager Valerie Simmons waved from behind the counter. Laura Hudson stood with her, still wearing her coat.

"You just missed Penny," Valerie volunteered while Laura and Gammy hugged each other.

"I'm dropping off your newest barista before I run some errands." The sounds of a foreign language drew Wila's attention. At one of the back tables in the dining room, Brother Giuseppe sat with Matt, a novelist who hung out at Java's Palace on a regular basis. The members of Mrs. Langston's knitting club shot occasional looks in the men's direction.

Wila turned back to Valerie. "What's going on with Matt and Giuseppe?"

Valerie lowered her voice. "Father McAvoy set up regular security during business hours. Matt's been working with Giuseppe on his English in return for a free breakfast."

"And the side-eyes from the knitting club?"

Valerie grinned. "After a couple of hours with Matt, Giuseppe teaches the Italian language to the ladies, and gives them history lessons."

Wila frowned. "Do they know—"

Valerie shook her head. "Only Matt and the staff know about his real past. Mrs. Langston and her friends know he's a monk, but we told them he's an Italian professor teaching at UC-Oakfield."

Wila sighed. "As long as they know he's off limits."

"Okay, ladies." Valerie clapped her hands. "Let's get you some aprons and get that paperwork filled out."

"See you later, Gammy!"

Her grandmother gave her an absent wave as she followed Valerie and Laura down the hallway to the office. The same pang hit her heart as earlier with Derek short goodbye. Was she doomed to have everyone she loved leave her?

"You want your large white chocolate mocha, Ms. Ardale?" Alan's bright, genuine smile and blond all-American looks brought him a ton of tips, but there was a shadow behind his eyes since he had been possessed last month. He claimed he didn't remember anything, but that didn't mean the poor kid wasn't having nightmares.

She smiled and nodded. "Yes, please. And a chocolate croissant, too, but don't warm it up."

"Will do." He nodded.

A couple of minutes later, Wila was headed for the hospital and munching on her chocolate croissant. The pastry and mocha weren't healthy for her waistline, but they were perfect for her anxiety after last night's kissing episode and the flurry of texts about how to deal with Crucifer. Surprisingly, Coach Cordero had agreed to meet the Soccer Moms at Father McAvoy's hospital room. At least, the coach wasn't avoiding the subject of who he really was.

And Francine apologized for not coming clean to the rest of the Soccer Moms about Coach Cordero's real identity. She said she wasn't sure if she'd dreamed the whole incident of him saving her from falling into Hell, and she hadn't been sure of how to broach such a subject with him.

Damn. Wila's fingers trembled. She clenched them tighter around the steering wheel. Coach Cordero was the Second Coming, and that fact was not helping her PTSD one little bit. Maybe she needed that referral from Gene sooner rather than later.

But what the hell would she tell a shrink? *I'm the avatar of War, and my minivan turns into a horse. Oh, by the way, Jesus Christ coaches my son's soccer team.*

Her seat vibrated beneath her, Scarlett's attempt to comfort her. Wila pulled into a spot in the hospital's staff lot, shifted the gear into park, and leaned her forehead against the steering wheel.

The radio clicked on. "It . . . will be . . . all right, all right, all right . . . Wil . . . a."

She couldn't help but smile at her minivan/horse's reassurance. "I hope so, Scarlett, but I don't trust a demon farther than I can throw you."

"Ha. Ha-ha. Ha." Scarlett spun her radio through frequencies to find the right sounds. "Cruciferous vegetable . . . is . . . different."

Wila straightened. "How so?"

"He wants . . . to keep things . . . the way we were." Scarlett used Barbra Streisand's singing voice for the last phrase.

"Why?"

"Status quo . . . and . . . free will . . . means everyone wins a million dollars!"

"So he's looking at the long game?"

"You betcha, baby!"

Wila sat back in her seat and stared out the windshield, but she saw nothing beyond the glass. Scarlett made sense from a strategic point. A coup in Hell could avert the battle of the Apocalypse if the new prince brokered a peace treaty with Heaven.

But it would put millions, if not billions, of people at risk from demon possession and abuse. Could Coach Cordero and her sisters live with that kind of deal?

Could she?

Well, that question was the entire purpose of the meeting this morning.

"Do we need to move to a parking spot closer to your sisters?"

"That's . . . a . . . hell yes!" Scarlett answered through the radio.

Wila couldn't help smiling. "I assume you know where your sisters are."

"Hi-ho, Silver! . . . Knock three times . . . flooring on sale! Only half price!"

"Level Three in the parking garage. Got it." But before Wila could shift the gear, her minivan started rolling backwards. She slammed on the brake pedal. "Excuse me, but when you're a van, I do the driving. We've talked about this, Scarlett."

"I'm sorry. So sorry," the radio sang.

"Thank you." Wila shifted the gear into reverse and checked her mirrors and backup camera before she backed out of the space. Once on the third level, she couldn't miss the flashing yellow turn signals on the white minivan at the far end of the aisle. She pulled in next to Penny's minivan and patted the steering wheel. "You ladies have a nice time gossiping."

"Sharing a candybar . . . isn't . . . the worst thing . . . you could do."

Wila laughed. "Silly horse."

She grabbed her coffee and got out of the minivan. Penny's van had stopped flashing its turn signals. Her own vehicle's alarm beeped once, Scarlett's way of saying good luck. Funny how there were empty spots on either side of the pair of minivan/horses for Sable and Verde when the other two Soccer Moms arrived. She wished she knew how they did it. That talent would come in handy when she ran errands.

After two elevator rides and a lot of walking, Wila finally made it to Father McAvoy's room. The coach and Father Perez leaned against the wall, underneath the TV. Father Mbaye sat in the visitor chair close to the bed. Penny perched on the couch.

"Dammit, Wila, I brought you coffee." Penny's eyebrows drew together in an angry "V" on her forehead.

"I didn't get off my shift until midnight, and I couldn't get to sleep until after three, so I'm working on less than four hours of rest here." Wila made a point of gulping down the remainder of her cup and tossed the cardboard into the trash can by the door. "See? I'm ready for the next one."

The coach shook his head and made *tsk*ing sounds. "We're going to get our asses kicked out of the hospital if you folks get rowdy."

"I wood ike oo ged kid oud," Father McAvoy grumbled.

"Still having a little trouble with language, Father?" Wila moved closer to the hospital bed. "I thought the ER got a line for the tPA run in time."

"His articulation is a lot better than it was yesterday," Father Mbaye said. "Mobility is good. Eyesight's returned. Still a little weakness in the grip of his left hand. The occupational therapist has already been here, and a speech therapist is supposed to visit later this afternoon."

"Sounds like you're in good hands, Padre." Wila smiled at the elderly priest.

A mischievous twinkle gleamed in his eyes. "I had oo impose, Wia, bud wood you breed me a shake from Wison's?"

"Sure. What flavor?"

"Kokwade, pease."

Francine entered the hospital room. "I hope we haven't missed everything."

Dani followed her inside and closed the door, but she held onto the handle a bit longer than necessary before she turned and faced the group.

Wila cocked her head. "Everything okay, girl?"

"Depends on what you mean. I killed—" Dani made bunny ears with her index and middle fingers on both hands. "—the oil in the latch to buy us some time before one of the staff comes in." She grimaced. "Just to warn all of you, Courtney wasn't the only one recording us last night."

"What do you mean?" Penny asked.

Dani strode over and sat next to Penny before she pulled her phone from her shoulder bag. "I mean I got a blackmail threat by email." She tapped the screen a couple of times. Wila's voice burst from the speaker, shouting at Courtney to stop filming the Soccer Moms.

Oh, shit. Wila buried her face in her hands. Beside her, Francine murmured an obscenity Wila didn't think Miz Perfect even knew.

"From the angle, it could have been one of the refs filming it," Penny commented.

"Or one of the police officers," Dani said. "It's about the right angle for one of their body cams.

"No one there last night was possessed except for Crucifer being in Chance Paxton's body," Coach Cordero said.

Wila looked up as he crossed to the couch to peer over Dani's shoulder at the video she was showing to Penny.

"Do you know who sent it?" Francine asked.

Dani shook her head. "It's some random ColdMail account."

"You mentioned blackmail?" Father Perez frowned. "What do they want?"

"A million dollars," Dani said dryly.

"Oh, is that all?" Sarcasm dripped from Penny's tone.

Wila looked at Francine.

"I don't have that kind of cash lying around!" she protested.

"Chill, girl. None of us do," Wila replied.

"What do they plan to do if you don't comply?" Father Perez asked.

"Exactly what Courtney was threatening to do last night," Dani said. "Send the video to all the metro area news outlets."

Despite the anxiety racing through her, Wila said, "Then let them."

Chapter 11

Everyone stared at Wila in shock.

Penny was the first to get her voice back. "Are you insane?"

Wila shrugged. "Why not go public? Every human and demon around us are threatening to expose us as the Four Horsemen of the Apocalypse."

"Don't you mean the Four Soccer Moms of the Apocalypse?" Coach Cordero said with a grin.

Wila ignored him. "If we go public, it will stop the bullshit. Famine has already been exposed thank to the vigilantes at the Oakfield Cemetery three weeks ago. The mayor and the area LEOs know about Penny, Dani, and the demon hunters. What if we go on the offensive?" She turned to Francine. "Do you have the name and number of the guy who produces Neal's TV ads?"

Francine nodded. "Andy Gleeson. Do you have something in particular in mind?"

Wila waved nonchalantly. "If we pay to run the ad where we tell the public the truth, the reporters will come to us instead of chasing you. And it takes away the power of those threatening to expose us."

"Why pay?" Dani asked. "All we'd have to do is post it on social media."

"That's a much better idea," Penny said.

"The Church won't condone something like this," Father Perez protested.

"The Church also refused to send you aid when you and Deke requested it, Victor." Father Mbaye motioned to include the Soccer Moms. "If they wish to try their idea, who are we to stop them?"

Wila looked at Coach Cordero. She couldn't think of him as anything else. Otherwise, she wouldn't be able to do any of her jobs. "Is it safe to assume you don't want to be a part of this?"

He rubbed his chin. "As much as I want to support you, my public admission would cause all of us more problems than help you."

"Why include Jesus in this ad?" Father Perez used the Spanish pronunciation. He looked at them with a puzzled expression.

"Crap." The spot between Wila's brows ached and she rubbed it to ease the physical tension. "You haven't told them, have you?"

"We haven't gotten to that particular point of the discussion yet." The merriment in the coach's eyes would have been annoying if she weren't in on the joke. "We were sidetracked by the blackmail attempt."

"Od us whad?" Father McAvoy demanded.

Dani grinned at Father Perez. "Let's just say Christ has been hiding in plain sight this whole time."

"He, huh, what . . . noooo." The last syllable was rather drawn out as the padre's brain caught up with reality. The change of expression on his face was priceless. He dropped to his knees. "My Lord."

Father Mbaye simply stared at the coach. On the other hand, Father McAvoy laughed his ass off until he started coughing.

Wila grabbed the standard issue hospital sippy cup and helped the senior priest to sit upright and take a few swallows of water.

He gently pushed her hand back when he was done. "Thank you, my dear." He chuckled some more before he added, "Part of me wondered if I'd meet our Lord and Savior this week. This was not what I was expecting." His eyes widened, and he stuck out his tongue and twirled it around a few times. "Did I speak clearly?"

Wila nodded.

Father McAvoy smiled at the coach. "Do I have you to thank, my Lord?"

Coach Cordero shrugged. "The ladies need you. No, they didn't ask me for anything. And please call me, Jesus." He looked down at Father

Perez. "Victor, please get off the floor. We're friends, and you're making this weird."

Father Perez rose, but he still couldn't meet the coach's gaze.

Wila glanced over at Father Mbaye. He was still frozen in the visitor chair, still staring at the coach.

"Well, now that we've got that particular revelation out of the way—" Penny smiled. "Is everyone ready for their coffees?"

The three priests weren't much help. Not even when Father Mbaye finally came out of his shellshock. There wasn't any mention of a Crucifer in any of the texts they'd read or heard of. Father Mbaye even called Father Lambert, who passed word through the rectory. Not even the oldest of the demon hunters, a Templar Knight from the First Crusade, had a clue of who Crucifer was.

All the coach would say was Crucifer was Satan's right-hand during the Battle and the Fall. Nothing he said was new information about Satan and his cronies. But the coach looked so damn sad, it tugged on Wila's heart.

Wila crossed her arms. "Scarlett says Crucifer's offer is genuine. What have the other horses said?"

"Verde can't figure out his end game," Dani said. "She says Satan makes more sense."

"Why does he make more sense?" Francine said.

"Let me guess. Daddy issues?" Penny quipped.

The coach laughed. "You could say that. Is Gene taking new patients?"

"Since he doesn't believe in you or Satan, I'd say he'd probably would." Penny grinned.

Wila laughed. "Please tell me you haven't told him about the coach."

"Are you kidding?" Penny scoffed. "I am not that insane."

"Sable agrees Crucifer is being honest with us, but she's worried Satan knows about Crucifer's plan to double-cross him," Francine said.

Penny raised her hands. "I haven't asked Silver, but I will." She stood. "Are we done here? I've got a business to run."

"Um, there's one more thing before you leave," Coach Cordero said.

Wila tensed, half-afraid of what new disaster was about to be dumped on her and her sisters.

Coach Cordero's left eyebrow rose. "Is it all right if Maria still joins your girl's night?"

"Of course, it is!" Wila blurted. "Why wouldn't it be?"

He shrugged. "She was afraid after learning our real identities last night, you ladies might be reluctant to associate with her."

Wila laughed. "If we held anyone's husband against them, we would have kicked out Francine ages ago."

"What?" Francine glared at her.

"By the way, thank you for whatever you said or did to get Neal to ditch that atrocious rug he wore." Wila grinned.

"I wouldn't be complaining about my husband if I were you," Francine grumbled.

"Point being—" Wila turned back to Coach Cordero. "Maria is always welcome at our girls' nights."

He smiled and nodded. "I'll tell her, but it would mean more coming from one of you."

Wila pulled her phone out of her jeans pocket and quickly typed a text. "Done. Anything else?"

Everyone shook their heads.

"Then I need to get a chocolate milkshake for a kindly priest," Wila said. "And then I need to run the sweeper through my house before my guests arrive." She paused with her hand on the door lever. "Assuming my dead grandmother hasn't already done all my chores while I was in the shower this morning."

She tugged on the lever. It didn't budge. She pressed her lips together to keep from shouting obscenities and counted to ten in German before she turned around to face the others. "Dani? We can't get out of the room."

"Let me." Coach Cordero crossed to the door as Wila stepped out of the way. He turned the lever and pulled the door open. "There you go."

"Thanks." Wila nodded. "Tell Maria we'll see her tonight."

It only took a few minutes to retrieve her minivan and pick up a chocolate shake for the hospitalized Father McAvoy, though he'd probably be released in the morning. In anticipation of someone staying at the hospital with him, she bought two. By the time she returned to the Oakfield Hospital, all of the priest's guests had left except Father Mbaye.

And Father McAvoy was sound asleep.

"The . . . coach said he would sleep through the afternoon," Father Mbaye whispered.

"I wish the coach had said something to me before I got the milkshake for Father McAvoy." Wila handed the second cup to Father Mbaye.

Father McAvoy snorted before he peered up at Wila. "I was resting my eyes, waiting for you to bring me my treat." He sighed as she gave the shake to him. "Fifty years ago, Ed said Wilson's had the best shakes in the world. I have to admit he's right."

"You gentlemen enjoy your milkshakes. You got my number if you need anything."

Ten minutes later, Wila pulled into the Arrow parking lot to buy the items she hadn't purchased Monday morning. Tension yanked on her muscles, and anxiety sizzled along her nerves. She waited for Crucifer or any other demon to pop around the endcap of every aisle she pushed her cart down. Even worse, she constantly looked over her shoulders.

She was definitely disturbing the white suburban moms who were also shopping. She pursed her lips. Tough. They might as well join her in crazy town.

Wila paid for the toilet paper, tampons, and all the other mundane crap of modern life. Cold rain sprinkles rearranged the dust coating Scarlett while Wila loaded the bags in the back of the minivan. But the gray clouds did nothing more than spit.

"Sorry, baby. I'll take you for a bath tomorrow morning," Wila murmured.

"Can I join you both?"

At the deep masculine voice, Wila gritted her teeth and gently touched the close button for the back hatch before she turned to face Crucifer.

Chapter 12

Wila shifted to keep the shopping cart between her and the demon. "What do you want? You said we had forty-eight hours to make our decision."

He shrugged. "I thought I'd check if you'd decided early after your big meeting at the hospital."

Wila squeezed the handle of the cart with both sets of her fingers. The Soccer Moms didn't need any more uncontrolled publicity by her manifesting her sword in public again. "Worried your boss will find out you're planning on screwing him over?"

"Would it surprise you if I said yes?"

"Maybe it would be in our best interest to tell him," Wila taunted.

Crucifer laughed. "Then I won't be the only one having their privates fried off in Hell."

"I thought angels didn't have junk, Broccoli." She shot him a sly smile, praying her nerves didn't show. "Whether they are Fallen or not."

Crucifer matched her expression. "Now, how could we have knocked up the daughters of man if we didn't have the plumbing to do the job?"

"By stealing a human body, like you're doing right now." She gestured to indicate the poor lawyer he currently possessed.

He gave an amused snort before he gave her the once over. "Care to put your assumptions to the test, War?"

She shook her head. "I don't have the time or inclination to carry Rosemary's baby."

"It might make the next day of waiting a little more . . . pleasurable," he purred.

"Look, Bok Choy, harassing me, much less the other Soccer Moms, won't make things go faster." Wila cocked her head. "In fact, I think you set us up at the park last night. For all I know, you're the one who sent the extortion e-mail to Death."

"Extortion e-mail?" He actually tried to look confused. "How on earth could I threaten Boss Baby, much less his harem of Amazons? Besides, darling, demons are much more successful when we stay under Heavenly and human radar."

"You mean like how Seth Rimmon tried to stay under our radar?" Wila didn't want to admit she was pretty sure a human videoed her threatening Courtney last night, but she might as well do some poking to see what she could get out of Crucifer.

The demon sighed. "That boy may have been bucking for a promotion, but he didn't have the brains or experience to pull it off. Kidnapping? Death threats? For what? The end result was him, his entire team, and any other demon he sucked into his scheme are now dead, and the Horsemen—" He smirked. "Sorry, the Soccer Moms of the Apocalypse and the Kid know of our presence before we were ready."

"So your prince sent you to clean up Rimmon's mess?"

Crucifer shrugged. "Someone had to."

"Why did you kill him? And Janet Little?"

"He killed the human cow when she outlived her usefulness. And the skin he wore before Pestilence killed him? Well, it remembered too much."

She stared at Crucifer. "You could have let him go. He wasn't a threat to you. If he tried to tell anyone the truth, he would have ended up in a mental hospital."

"Depends on your definition of threat, my dear."

Was that remorse Wila saw in his eyes? No, it couldn't be. He was a demon. He may have been an angel at one time, but he wasn't anymore.

"Why are you helping us, Crucifer?"

He shrugged again. "The throne, of course."

"No." The calm of her mediation techniques settle over her, and she could see both the angel he was and the demon he'd become. "That's not the truth. At least, it's not the whole truth." She sighed and shook her head. "If you want us to trust you, you're going to have to tell us eventually."

He opened his mouth and closed it before his devious smile returned. "I'll see you tomorrow night, War. Have fun at your girls' night." He sauntered across the parking lot.

Something wasn't right, and Wila wished she could put her finger on what was really bothering her about this whole situation.

The question still bugged Wila over the next hour and a half while she stopped at the dry cleaners, the post office, and the pet store to pick up Martin and Malcolm's specialty food. But the worry was replaced with suspicion when Wila and Scarlett pulled into the driveway. A forest green late model Honda Accord sat on the left side of the concrete. Except no one Wila knew drove such an older vehicle. Not in Oakfield. And none of her relatives still living in Chicago would bother with a non-American car.

After the weird talk with Crucifer in the Arrow parking lot, she wasn't about to open the garage door and invite a different demon inside her home. "You sensing anything, Scarlett?"

"Human nature," the radio sang.

Scarlett's analysis pointed out part of what had been bugging Wila. She hadn't sensed Crucifer during each encounter until she saw him or he spoke to her. If he knew how to hide himself, other demons in Oakfield might have the same talent, too.

"Are you sure?" Wila asked Scarlett.

"I'm only human," the radio sang.

Wila sucked in a deep breath and stepped out of the minivan. The other driver exited her Accord at the same time and crossed in front of her car. Raspberry streaks highlighted her dark brunette pixie cut. She wore jeans, a leather jacket, and boots and carried the same confident air as Karen and the other demon hunters.

"Are you Wila Ardale?"

"That depends on who's asking."

"Don't play games with me, girlfriend. I'm just the delivery person."

Wila clenched her fists. "I'm not your girlfriend. And you could have left the package at the door."

"So your grandmother could destroy it and claim it wasn't left there?" The other woman's pierced eyebrow rose.

A sinking feeling threatened to squeeze Wila's heart out between her toenails. "Then quit playing games with me. If you're a process server, hand over the papers and be done with it."

The woman reached into her jacket and pulled out not one, but two manila envelopes. "Thanks for not acting like a bitch about this."

"Like you said, you're only the messenger." Wila took the envelopes from the woman's outstretched hand.

She waited until the process server climbed into her sedan, backed out of the drive, and took off down the street before she looked at the first envelope. Sure enough, it was from the ex-louse's divorce attorney. But her blood chilled at the law firm listed on the second envelope. The ex-louse's employer. What kind of game was he playing now?

Wila turned to open the minivan door in order to hit the button on the garage door opener clipped to the visor. Scarlett decided to shift into horse mode and phased into the garage. She probably thought she was helping Wila, but it was damn annoying when a minivan had a mind of her own.

At least, Wila had the presence of mind to grab her keys when she climbed out of the minivan. She stalked over to her front door and unlocked it.

To find Sister Joan standing by the front blinds with a gun in her hand.

"Thank God, you're home," she said in her elegant English accent as she holstered her weapon. Malcolm stood behind her, extending and retracting his claws.

"Baby girl, there was a car sitting in your driveway most of the afternoon—" Gammy started.

"She's a process server, and she's gone." Wila tossed her purse on the loveseat. Martin jumped on top of the back and rubbed his head against her. She skritched behind his ears. "I'm assuming she wasn't here when you brought Gammy home from Java's Palace, Sister."

The nun shook her head.

"Process server?" Gammy clutched the edges of her housecoat. "What did you do?"

"I divorced my cheating husband."

Martin meowed in protest when Wila ripped open the first envelope and scanned the contents. Sure enough, the ex-louse was suing for full custody of Derek and asked for an emergency custody order. The hearing on the emergency order was scheduled for first thing in the morning. "And now, he claims my dead grandmother living here is a danger to his son."

"What? I'd never hurt a hair on any of my grandbabies' heads!" Gammy grabbed the paperwork from Wila's hands.

Bitter laughter poured from Wila. "Gammy, he's a piece of work. I just didn't see it in time." It was the least offensive thing she could call the ex-louse without lectures on language and manners from her grandmother and the resurrected nun. Wila ripped open the second envelope and pulled out the paperwork. At the name on top of the page and the attorney's signature, she couldn't stop herself from launching a stream of obscenities.

She yanked her phone out of her pocket and tapped the call icon for Penny's number.

"Hello?"

"You should have gone after the bitch for slapping you, Penny. Courtney Lasser just sued me for threatening her. And she hired my ex-husband to do it!"

Chapter 13

Wila breathed heavily waiting for a response from her friend. She need-ed someone rational to talk her down, and Penny Hudson was the most rational person she knew.

Penny's groan rattled the phone speaker. "Give me a minute."

In the background, Wila could hear Penny's assistant manager Valerie taking orders. While Wila waited, Malcolm joined his brother on the love-seat. The two cats meowed softly to each other.

Wila glanced at the time on her phone and squelched the urge to text Derek to tell him she would pick him up. That would violate the current custody agreement, and she knew damn well the ex-louse would use such a move against her.

That didn't mean fear didn't squeeze her heart at the thought of never seeing her son again.

The noise at the other end of the line faded, which meant Penny had retreated to her office at Java's Palace. A chair squeaked before Penny said, "I take it you were served with the lawsuit after we left the hospital?"

"Tell her about Deion's other stunt, too," Gammy demanded.

"What else did the ex-louse do?" Penny asked.

Wila switched the phone to speaker mode. "I'll tell the three of you everything, but I need you to keep any commentary to yourselves until I'm done."

"Of course," Penny said. Gammy and Sister Joan nodded.

Wila sat down on the loveseat while Gammy and the nun/demon

hunter settled on the couch. The two Siamese purred and rubbed their heads against Wila in an effort to comfort her. She ran through every encounter she suffered through after she left the chocolate milkshakes with the priests at the hospital. Penny gasped at the mention of Crucifer, but otherwise, she remained silent. Wila ended with the process server handing her the notice of the two lawsuits.

"Have you called Lilah yet?" Penny asked.

Wila laughed bitterly. "Girl, I haven't taken off my coat yet, much less brought in my bags from the store."

"Then get your stuff out of Scarlett's ass, put it away, hang up your coat, and make yourself a cup of coffee," Penny said. "Preferably, decaf."

"I've got to clean the kitchen and bathrooms for tonight—" Wila stared at the living room floor, finally noticing the perfectly perpendicular vacuum marks on the carpet.

"As long as the ice maker's working and you have toilet paper, none of us give a rat's ass about your house," Penny said. "And if you don't have ice or toilet paper, tell me now, and I'll bring them."

Gammy and Sister Joan giggled.

Wila glared at the women on her couch. "What did you two do?"

"We got bored." Gammy glanced at her co-conspirator. "We decided we'd clean the house, then watch *Magic Mike* for our reward."

"I finished up in the kitchen while Latricia took a shower." Sister Joan grinned.

Penny roared with laughter over the phone at the idea of two resurrected elderly women watching hot guys gyrate on the TV screen.

Wila closed her eyes. With everything that had happened today, this was the proverbial last straw on her back.

"Gammy, make sure you and Sister Joan watch *Magic Mike XXL*, too," Penny said between chuckles. "The scene with Joe Manganiello in the convenience store is soooo worth it."

Wila's eyes snapped open. "You're not helping."

"Who's Joe Manganiello?" Sister Joan asked.

"Oh, dear." Gammy made a face. "He's a little after your time. I'll introduce you to *True Blood* tomorrow. He has a lot of shirtless scenes in that show, too. Or at least he did in the last season I watched. We should have Laura join us for a marathon!"

"I don't know what's worse—my son hitting puberty or two horny senior citizens in my living room," Wila said to Penny. "I'll see you tonight." She ended the call and stood. "You two have fun with your movies. I need to talk to my attorney."

An hour and a half later, Wila laid down her phone on the kitchen table and rose to brew her third cup of coffee.

Bless her attorney, Lilah said to let her take care of the ex-louse, but she wasn't as positive about the lawsuit by Courtney since the last time she tried a tort case was twenty years ago. Wila had thirty days to file an answer. Lilah would make some calls this afternoon about alternate representation for Courtney's case and discuss the possibilities with Wila after the hearing tomorrow morning.

It wasn't the answer Wila wanted, but it would have to do. For now.

Unfortunately, there was one more call she needed to make. While her little coffee maker chugged away, she retrieved her phone and dialed the number for the station. Her hands shook. She'd never asked for special favors before, but she couldn't lose Derek. She kept her sanity together for him. He needed one parent who could.

After the first ring, the captain picked up. "Miller."

"Captain, were you serious about me calling if there's an issue and I need time off?"

"Just a sec." A couple of seconds later the background noise faded, and he said, "Go ahead, Wila."

"My ex just served me with papers for an emergency custody hearing for tomorrow morning." She swallowed hard. "I don't know how long it's going to take."

The captain snorted. "Let me guess. Jackson found out about your extracurricular activities."

"If he did, he didn't mention it in his motion." Wila sighed. "He's claiming my grandmother constitutes a threat to Derek's health and well-being."

"Miz Latricia?" Captain Miller roared, but when his laughter abruptly died, he said, "I apologize. It can't be funny to you."

"It is . . . ridiculous." A bitter chuckle welled up.

A knocking sound came from the speaker, and the captain yelled, "Come in."

Muffled men's voices filtered over the line before the captain said, "Jensen can cover for you in return for a box of Long Johns. That acceptable?"

Wila smiled. She'd covered for Jensen quite a bit when his wife and their newborn girl were in the hospital from complications during her birth. When he tried to make it up to her, she only asked for a box of Long Johns from The Bake Shoppe. "That would be more than acceptable, sir. I'll see you Friday."

A huge weight lifted from her shoulders. A weight she hadn't realized was sitting there. She shoved her phone into her jeans pocket.

Once the coffee maker spit out the last drops, she picked up her cup, added a healthy dollop of white chocolate syrup, and headed into the living room. Martin and Malcolm perched on the two middle stairs and peered at Gammy and Sister Joan through the bannister. The two women shrieked like a couple of teenagers at the antics on screen.

Gammy thumbed the pause button on the remote. "What's wrong, baby girl?"

"I have to be in court tomorrow morning." Wila sat on the loveseat, weary to the bone. "There's an emergency hearing for temporary custody of Derek."

"Then I'm coming with you," Gammy stated.

"Could your ex-husband be possessed by a demon?" Sister Joan asked.

"I wish I could say that." Wila sighed. "But this is pure, unadulterated ex-louse spite."

"I hope you're not calling Deion names in front of Derek," Gammy said. "I understand the man hurt you something fierce, but he's still your son's father. You can't make Derek choose between you and Deion."

"I don't call him names in front of Derek." Wila sipped her coffee. "And I don't make Derek choose between us. You were a convenient excuse to cause trouble, and my ex-husband is angry our son defied him Sunday night, even though Derek himself adhered to the custody order."

She took another sip and settled back against the comfortable upholstery. Deion had been so worried about appearances. The furniture he demanded when they were together was the latest in interior design, but it had been as uncomfortable as hell. She had been ecstatic to leave it all to him during the divorce.

Gammy and Sister Joan looked at each other before they both turned back to Wila.

"We're coming to court with you tomorrow," Gammy declared again.

"In fact, we could get everyone at the rectory to come to court as well," Sister Joan added.

"And you know your sisters will come." The expression on Gammy's face dared Wila to challenge her.

"If any of you argue with the judge or piss her off, I will go War on your asses." Wila glared at the pair. "You feel me?"

They both nodded.

"Good." Wila kicked off her shoes and tucked her feet under her on the loveseat. "How was your first day at Java's Palace, Gammy?"

"I wasn't expecting homework, but it was a lot more fun than I thought it would be." Gammy smiled.

"Homework?"

"All the drink recipes," Gammy said. "But Penny doesn't want me back until Friday afternoon."

"Don't worry," Sister Joan assured Wila. "I'll help her study tomorrow morning before we head to the courthouse and after you go to work."

Wila shook her head. "I already called my captain. I have tomorrow off for the hearing, and whatever else—" She stopped herself from calling him her favorite pet name. "—Deion manages to throw at me. What if I ask Francine if you can practice on her espresso machine?"

"I don't want to be a bother," Gammy protested. "I only need to memorize the recipes."

"You'll get it, Gammy. I'm sorry I don't have the energy to go car shopping today. I have Saturday off. We'll go down and look at the used cars at Neal's dealership." Wila sipped her coffee. "For now, let's finish *Magic Mike*. Penny's right. The second one is a lot more fun, and we can fit it in before our guests arrive."

Chapter 14

Malcolm and Martin had raced upstairs when Francine arrived with Karen. There were simply too many humans for the felines' comfort.

Wila was still surprised how much their girls' night had grown over the last six weeks. The only thing weirder was the get together now consisted of her dead grandmother, three demon hunters, and the wife of Christ in addition to the four Soccer Moms of the Apocalypse.

That bizarre thought and the lawsuits proved how much she really needed a vacation.

After she told everyone the results of her conversation with Lilah, and they all pledged to come to the hearing tomorrow, Wila's guests settled down to play cards and discuss both Wila's legal situation and Dani's blackmailer.

Since they had too many people now for even teams to play euchre, they'd switched to poker. Sister Joan shook her head as she studied the five cards in her hand. "I don't understand how this Courtney woman can sue you, Wila. You didn't threaten her. You told her to stop filming you. There's a huge difference." She tossed two wrapped truffles into the kitty. "One card."

"Seriously?" Karen wore a funky expression. "Sister, you do understand you're in the U.S.A., right?"

"Yes," the nun drawled. "But I still don't understand the basis of the lawsuit. In the United Kingdom, there is a right to privacy. Surely, the Unites States takes it further with your precious Constitution."

"What our very junior demon hunter is trying not to say—" Laura scooted two cards to Dani who had dealt this hand. "—Courtney is a Karen causing trouble." She tossed two truffles on the growing pile.

"Hey!" Karen protested. "What have I said about using my name as a slur?"

Sister Joan's frown deepened. "How is the name Karen now an insult?"

"The term Karen means she's a white woman with a certain conservative view, many times a certain haircut, and either blonde or with highlights, who enjoys causing trouble for those she believes are beneath her social status out of spite," Wila said. "The behavior is often aimed at people of color because of racism."

"Another sensitivity training at the station?" Penny said sympathetically.

"Every time Miles Pence opens his dang mouth." Wila decided to mess with the other girls, raised the bet by three truffles, and asked for two cards. She already held three of a kind, king high. Maybe she'd get lucky and pull the fourth one. Dani handed over two cards. Nope, still three of a kind. "On the other hand, our Karen may be white, but her hair is blue, she can kick demon ass, and she's not a bigot."

"So, is this American slang, or is it a new term?" Sister Joan asked.

"Both." Dani laid down two cards and matched Wila's wager. "A pair for me. Bet's to you, Maria."

She didn't bat an eyelash. "I see Wila and raise another three truffles." She didn't ask for any cards.

Francine whistled and folded. "Too rich for me."

"I'm with Blondie." Gammy laid her hand down as well.

"Out." Penny grimaced, but it was a toss-up whether it was her bad hand or her phone buzzing. She pulled the device out of her pocket, checked her text, and smiled. "I'm on for court tomorrow."

"You need to give all your employees raises," Wila muttered.

"I've already given them bonuses for getting possessed by demons," Penny said dryly. "What more do you want?"

"My ex-husband and Courtney Lasser to magically disappear." Wila eyed Karen. "Bet's to you, Longstreet."

Karen took a sip of her electric lemonade while she contemplated her hand. "I think you shouldn't put wishes like that out into the universe. I see both raises and raise one more." She tossed the requisite truffles onto the pile.

Wila frowned at the hunter. "What's that supposed to mean?"

"You've got a demon trying to make a deal with the Four Soccer Moms." Karen laid down her cards. "What if Crucifer decides to kill your ex-husband and this Courtney as a favor to you? With two ongoing lawsuits, who do you think the police are going to look at first?"

"She's right, baby girl," Gammy murmured.

Sister Joan knocked on the table twice to indicate she folded. Laura did the same.

"Here's more food for thought." Wila exhaled before she tossed five truffles in the kitty. "Did anyone else sense Crucifer before Dani spotted him leaning against my rig last night?"

"No." The alarmed expression on Dani's face scared Wila more than her actual answer. They both looked at Francine and Penny. The two exchanged looks before they both turned back to Wila and shook their heads.

"Crap." Wila took a huge gulp of her drink before she added, "I was really hoping it was only my demon radar that was screwed up."

"What do you mean by demon radar?" Sister Joan asked.

"We know when demons are nearby," Penny said.

Francine made a face. "It's pretty accurate within a quarter of a mile. We should have known Crucifer was outside the soccer field last night."

"Long before we saw him," Dani added.

Penny leaned her elbows on the table. "Same thing happen to you at Arrow? You didn't sense him at all?"

Wila nodded. "Both Monday and today."

Maria laid down her cards, concern etching lines on her forehead. "You need to be carrying holy water at all times, *chica*. Jesus wasn't joking when he said Crucifer is nearly as powerful at the Morningstar."

"So, why not use his invisibility screen to kill us?" Wila laid down her own cards. "He's got the upper hand. We can't keep him out of the fire station, Java's Palace, or Dani's office. Why not walk in before we know he's there?" She made gun fingers and aimed them at her own head. "Boom. Execute us. We're out of the way. Demons win."

"I doubt it's that simple," Francine said softly.

"It's not," Maria added. "There are rules."

"Then what are the rules, Maria?" Wila glared at the woman. "We're handicapped here because we don't understand what the hell is happening!"

"You can only fight them in open battle, and the demons must do the same." Maria's sad expression made Wila want to cry. "As you have done twice before."

"What about the demon who possessed Seth Rimmon?" Penny asked.

Maria shrugged. "You didn't touch him until he stole your daughter and your employees."

"But Edward threw holy water on Demon Seth's partner during Penny's negotiations with Demon Seth at dinner?" Francine said.

"A human demon hunter tossed the glass of water at her, not one of us," Dani commented thoughtfully.

"Exactly." Maria nodded.

"So, I can't just stab Crucifer with my flaming sword if he stalks me through a store again?" Wila reached for her own glass and sipped the electric lemonade.

"Not while you are under negotiations." Maria lifted her chin. "Which is what happened when Penny asked for forty-eight hours to consider his proposal."

"In other words, I should have stabbed the bastard Monday morning before he made the offer," Wila grumbled.

"Is that what you want to be? A murderer?" Maria wore the same disappointed look Coach Cordero had the day Penny's daughter decked little Kenny Lasser after he called her a slut for getting her period.

"Wila!" Gammy stared at her in horror. "Would you murder someone, anyone, in cold blood? Like someone did to your mother and brother?"

Of course, she brought *that* subject up. Francine, Penny, and Dani stared at Wila with varying degrees of horror and sorrow. She had only told Penny to the truth about her mom and brother's deaths. From Dani's expression, she'd guessed the truth. And Francine wore the typical white woman sympathy for the poor little Black girl.

"No!" Wila threw up her hands. "But is there a difference between a gang drive-by and killing a demon? Am I going to Hell already for killing demons who kidnapped Justine? How is that any different than shish ke-babbing any random demon like Crucifer?"

"Did you ever make the first move?" Sister Joan asked.

"What do you mean the first move?" Penny responded.

"Did you attack a demon before it tried to harm you or an innocent?" Laura asked.

Wila and Penny stared at each other before they glanced at Francine and Dani.

"The closest any of us came to doing something like that is when I shot the possessed driver fleeing Saint Michael's," Penny said.

"That's not even close." Maria smiled at them all. "You and Father Perez came to my rescue when those two demons were sent to murder me."

"Well, shoot." Wila rested her chin on her palm. "I guess that means I have to put up with Crucible and his smarmy come-ons, instead of stabbing him."

"Sounds like he wants to do the stabbing." Francine smirked. "How long has it been for you, Wila?"

Wila flipped a double bird at Francine.

"Wila!" Gammy scolded.

The other six women laughed hysterically.

"Maybe we should call it a night if we're all attending court tomorrow." Laura wiped her eyes.

"No, ma'am. We are finishing this hand first." Wila tossed a truffle into the kitty. "I see Karen."

Dani folded her cards. "I'm out."

Maria pushed four truffles into the pile. "Raise you by three, Karen."

The demon hunter tapped her cards against the table before she shook her head. "I am not challenging the most favored disciple of Christ. Out."

Wila pushed her last three truffles into the pot. "Call."

Maria laid down her cards. Wila's mouth fell open, and she stared at the three aces.

"There's a reason Simon Peter didn't like me." Maria chuckled while she collected her winnings. "The children at the community center will love your contributions, ladies."

"This hearing tomorrow means I need to cancel our initial meeting with Andy," Francine said. "By the way, what are we planning to do about Dani's blackmailer?"

Willa turned to Dani. "How long did they give you?"

"Midnight tomorrow night," she replied.

"Screw 'em." Wila shook her head. "The mayor, the police, and every religious leader in Oakfield know who we are. It's only a matter of time before everyone else in town finds out. We already have the video of Francine from October circulating."

"So, the consensus is for me to ignore the e-mail?" Dani looked at Penny and Francine. They both nodded.

"Good." Dani grinned. "I don't like bullies, and I don't want to give in to their stupid demands. Even if I actually had a million dollars."

"I'll reschedule our meeting with Andy," Francine said. "Anything else we need to worry about before tomorrow morning?"

The guests gave a chorus of negative replies. Thank goodness. Wila didn't think she could handle anymore chaos in her life right now.

Everybody helped clean up the kitchen, but Wila's attention was drawn to Sister Joan, Gammy, and Laura whispering in the family room. She grabbed the full trash bag and marched into the room.

"What are you three up to?"

Gammy and Laura displayed guilty faces, but Sister Joan tapped her chin with her index finger, wearing a thoughtful expression.

"Given this demon's special interest in you, it might be best to assign a hunter to you personally," the nun said.

"That's not a bad idea," Penny said from the kitchen.

"Mind your own business, Hudson," Wila snapped before she turned back to Gammy and the demon hunters. "How do you plan to do that? A paramedic ride-along? The captain isn't going to agree to let my bodyguard come with us on calls."

"Told ya she wasn't going to go for your plan," Karen said loudly.

"Baby girl, I don't want Derek growing up without a momma like you did," Gammy protested. "And I don't like the fact this demon is stalking you in particular."

"Because everyone knows I'm the weakest of the Four Soccer Moms," Francine yelled.

"The demons found out the hard way that's not true," Dani shouted.

"Is this how you guys discuss everything?" Maria joined in on the hollering.

"You all are giving me a headache!" Wila screamed. She turned to the three older women. "Quit making secret plans behind my back." She headed for the garage with the sack of trash, tossed it into the container—

And walked back into a generational war.

Wila rubbed the spot between her eyebrows as the three oldest women were animatedly arguing with the five younger women in her kitchen.

All over whether she needed a bodyguard.

No, she wasn't having the same argument twice in less than two minutes. She headed out the back door and took a deep breath of the cold air.

"Are they always so loud?"

Wila jumped and whirled to her right. Crucifer sat on the edge of one of her patio's elevated flower beds.

Chapter 15

The breeze rustled the dry, dead stems and leaves in the redwood bed. Any hint of fall was gone. The demon was actually wearing a wool dress coat. And the closed door barely muffled the arguing in Wila's kitchen.

She looked over her shoulder at her guests before she turned back to Crucifer. "I'm not the one stupid enough to sit in the cold and listen to a bunch of hens clucking."

"You said that," the demon muttered. "I didn't."

Wila crossed her arms. "If you came for an answer to your proposal, we don't have one."

"Yet." He smiled. Too bad the human in front of her was possessed. He did have a nice smile when the demon inside wasn't making smarmy remarks.

"Is that why you're out here? To eavesdrop?"

"Among other things."

"What other things?" she demanded.

He sighed, and the steam from his breath drifted away in the slight wind. "Primarily to keep other demons away."

She laughed. "And how do they plan to get inside my home?"

"Not inside. Destroy your house from the outside. You ladies make yourselves vulnerable when you collect in one place like this."

Damn. Of course, he came to one of the Soccer Moms' houses with no outside cameras or alarms. She needed to grab Karen for a little help getting the security system she bought installed tomorrow morning. The demon hunter could install another one at Dani's place in the afternoon.

But Wila's lack of outside security cameras still didn't answer why Crucifer was here.

"And you could attack each of us separately," she pointed out.

"Is that what you expect?"

"Isn't that why you're stalking me?"

"No."

Well, that tactic didn't work. Time for a new plan. "Why not use the cannon fodder to get rid of us? One of them might get lucky."

He snorted. "As lucky as the idiot Pestilence shot outside of Saint Michael's after he assaulted the most favored Disciple? Or Gakeel's nest who possessed Pestilence's staff? The random demons you and your sisters killed mere weeks into your roles? Or the lucky ten thousand Famine exiled back to Hell all by herself? I'm just brushing the surface. Given the exponential losses every time a demon is stupid enough to take on a Soccer Mom of the Apocalypse by herself, you could eliminate all the demons currently on Earth."

Wila smiled. "And then there's Death."

"And then there's Death," he agreed. "The prince would prefer her on his side."

That didn't sound good. Dani was a warm, sweet woman. There was only one thing the Devil could offer her to make her betray the human race. Had Heath already risen, and the demons captured him?

The last thing Wila needed was to give Crucifer any ideas. Time to change the subject.

"Is Gakeel the idiot who possessed Seth Rimmon?"

"Yes."

This was worse than playing Twenty Questions in the car with Derek. "Why on earth did Gakeel choose a two-bit conman like Rimmon?"

"Catnip." Crucifer grinned.

So, he'd been spying on the Soccer Moms since the beginning. Wila had to reign in her temper. She couldn't afford any more incidents. The

Fergusons, whose property bordered her backyard, had already asked about the sliced up, charred kitchen chair she'd left out here.

"That's not funny," she said. "I know you can only possess someone who's really scared or in a lot of pain."

"Rimmon got on the wrong side of a Chicago boss." Crucifer shrugged. "Gakeel saved him, but you won't give a mere demon any credit, will you?"

"That depends. What did Gakeel do to save Rimmon?"

"He removed a drug dealer from the streets."

Dammit. The demon knew what had happened to Mom and Watende, and he was using the information to get under her skin. Wila forced her muscles to relax and lowered her arms to her sides.

She laughed bitterly while she strolled over to the left elevated flower bed and perched on the edge. "Translation: your buddy murdered the mob boss and stole all his money to set Rimmon up as a legitimate businessman."

Crucifer eyed her. "Brilliant as well as beautiful and powerful. You are the entire package, my dear."

The abrupt change in his tactics killed her forced humor. "So, is this your way of engendering my trust? Giving me these lovely compliments?"

"I would never tell you what I really think," he murmured.

"I'd believe the insults before any sweet talk you spew."

"I know."

A shiver ran through her that had nothing to do with the cold. "What is that supposed to mean?"

"Never mind." Crucifer wouldn't meet her gaze. He stared at the dandelion growing from the space between two stones. Derek had begged Wila not to pull the weed. He claimed it showed resilience, just like the two of them. Now, its head was empty, but it looked healthier than any of the flowers she oh-so-carefully planted last spring.

"A hardy thing is a dandelion and so useful, but humans do not see its beauty," the demon murmured. "Not matter what is done to the plant, it merely digs its roots in deeper and survives." He looked up at her. "Which is why it's foolish to continue this war. It isn't about you or me. It never was. And I don't know about you, but I'm tired of dancing to Father's tune."

Too late. He was already under her skin. She hated she was beginning to feel a little sorry for him. "Isn't defying God what got you kicked out of Heaven along with the Devil?" she quipped.

He chuckled. "Ah, so when anger doesn't work as a defense, you resort to humor."

"It's not funny when your parent kicks you out of the house." She sighed.

"You sound like you're speaking from experience," Crucifer said.

Technically, Dad hadn't kicked her out of the house. He'd been so lost in his own grief he didn't realize for days Wila had moved in with Gammy.

"Let's focus on your problem for now." She cocked her head. "You've delivered your message about watching our backs. And your request for what you really want out of this deal—"

"Excuse me?" His eyebrows rose. "I made no such additional appeal."

Wila pushed to her feet. "Don't worry, Cabbage. I won't reveal your secret longing. However, I suggest you leave before the hunters inside realize you're out here. Their trigger fingers are a lot more itchy than the Soccer Moms."

The back door swung open, and Sister Joan stepped outside. "Wila, are you all right?"

"I didn't mean to worry you. I needed to cool off before I said something I regretted."

"We're sorry for making plans without discussing it with you first." The nun actually sounded contrite. "Please come back inside. It's freezing out here."

"All right." Wila looked at the other flower bed. Crucifer was gone, and she hadn't seen him leave. She crossed the flagstone patio. There was no sign the demon had even been there, except the scent of the expensive cologne either the demon or the man he possessed wore. A scent the breeze was quickly dissipating.

"Is something wrong?" Sister Joan asked.

"No." Wila stared into the night, but there was no hint of movement. "I saw something, but it turned out to be the Fergusons' cat. He must have slipped past whoever took the trash out." She shook her head before she turned back toward the nun. "The last six weeks of insanity is getting to me if I'm jumping at the neighbors' pets."

Wila followed Sister Joan back into the kitchen. Crucifer could be playing her just like Deion had. So why on earth did she believe the second-in-command of Hell was more honest with her than her ex-husband ever was?

Chapter 16

Nerves assailed Wila the next morning, long before her alarm buzzed. Remembering Lilah's advice from before, Wila pulled out the black suit she'd worn to Gammy's funeral years ago. The same suit she'd worn to court for her divorce and the previous custody hearings.

She had worried last night the skirt and jacket might not fit anymore. If anything, the fit was a little loose despite eating like a horse over the last couple of months. While she would've liked to blame Francine, it was probably the result of using her own powers plus the battles the Soccer Moms had fought. She'd lost weight in Afghanistan, too, despite the high calorie, high carb meals the Army served.

If she thought too much about her service, she'd totally lose it in front of the judge. Derek couldn't afford her breaking down. For all of Deion's rhetoric, his son was just another possession to him, not any more a real person than Wila.

A quick pass with the lint brush took care of the stray cat hairs on the wool fabric. She picked her curls into place, donned her conservative black headband, and examined her reflection. Her appearance didn't sit right. She'd changed since her divorce. She was War, the third Soccer Mom of the Apocalypse, dammit.

Wila removed the black headband and replaced it with the red one she often wore to work. And if she was going with her avatar's signature color, then she was going all the way. A little black eyeliner. A little ebony mascara. Then the piece de resistance. She slicked on her cherry red lipstick.

She blotted her lips and examined the effect before she smiled at her reflection. If the ex-louse wanted this fight, holy fire would rain on his head.

Downstairs, Gammy and Sister Joan waited for her on the couch. Both wore a white blouse and a black skirt, but the nun made a point of wearing her order's veil.

Gammy looked up as Wila descended the steps and grinned. "That's my baby girl."

Will grinned back. "Shall we go kick some ex-louse ass in court, ladies?"

Unfortunately, Scarlett wouldn't shut up on the drive to downtown. It was the first time she spoke in front of someone who wasn't a Soccer Mom. If the mare spoke with Derek, she sure didn't do it in front of Wila.

"I—can't—my knobs!" she cried from the speakers. "Stop! Stop! Stop!"

Gammy kept fiddling with the controls. "Baby girl, your radio is broken. Didn't you say you bought this minivan this year?"

A belt in the engine compartment whined.

"Gammy, stop messing with the radio controls," Wila admonished. "You're interrupting Scarlett while she's trying to tell me something."

"Oh!" Gammy jerked her hand back. "I'm so sorry, Scarlett. I forgot. I'm not used to a vehicle with a mind of her own."

"It's—all right, all right, all right," Scarlett replied. "What should—girl power—do—if—demons take over the world?"

"You and you sisters need to hold tight in the courthouse garage unless we call for you." Wila braked for a red light. "This is a human matter. I can't see the demons messing with something like a child custody hearing."

"Suspected confidence artist Seth Rimmon—in a court of law, there are two sides—take—your favorite beverage at Java's Palace," Scarlett sang the jingle for Penny's commercials. Wila thought they were a ridiculous waste of money, but Penny was right about people listening to the local radio stations on their way to work. The darn things had definitely paid for themselves.

"Yeah, I know Rimmon used the legal system to try to take the café from Penny, but this is a little different." The light changed to green, and Wila moved her foot to the accelerator.

"Caution!—Caution!—Caution!" Scarlett yelled.

"Lilah knows what she's doing, girl," Wila said. "I'll know if she, Deion's partner, or the judge have been compromised. We aren't going to be dealing with any new players, so please calm down."

"I'll be there for you," Scarlet crooned via a rock station.

"I know you will, and I appreciate it." Wila patted the dashboard.

"If it's any consolation, Scarlett, nearly every demon hunter from the rectory will be there to back up the Soccer Moms," Sister Joan said from the back seat. "No one's going to get away with taking Derek from Wila. Not even her ex-louse."

"Thank you—flying nun!"

Gammy giggled.

"You believe the sister, but you don't believe me?" Wila grumbled.

"We're a team!" Scarlett shot back. "Need to—protect—soccer moms."

"I swear, I'm not fighting with my minivan," Wila said through gritted teeth. Even Scarlett was getting on her last nerve, and that never happened. "Not today."

"Horse!" Scarlett yelled back through the speakers.

"That's enough out of both of you," Gammy snapped.

"Yes, ma'am," Willa and Scarlett said at the same time.

Everyone remained quiet for the rest of the ride to the courthouse. Wila turned into the parking garage. They were forty-five minutes early, but it was better than being late. Years ago, Wila had witnessed Judge Tellerson rip one husband a new one for showing up ten minutes after his hearing time. She doubted the judge had mellowed over the last few years.

Wila found some empty spots on the top floor close by the elevator. Once she pressed the stop button, she rested her hands on the dash. "Scarlett, I know you're picking up on my nerves, but you need to stay here unless

I call you. And only if I call you. I can't afford to piss off the judge today. This is her court, and I need to respect her authority. Do you understand?"

"Yes, my love." The radio squawked with static before Scarlett added, "Be-be-be—careful."

"We will. I promise." Wila patted the dashboard before she exited her minivan. Gammy and Sister Joan followed suit.

"You didn't lock your minivan," Gammy murmured while they walked toward the elevator. "I know Oakfield isn't the South Side, baby girl, but you still have crime here."

Wila snorted and press the down button. "Tell that to the kid who broke into Scarlett, after I locked her up, and is still sitting in County for grand theft auto."

Sister Joan emitted a sharp bark of laughter. "Did Scarlett punish the child?"

"Not directly," Wila admitted. The elevator doors opened, and the three women boarded the car.

"Unless you count scaring the shit out of the boy," Wila added while the elevator descended. "She locked him inside of the minivan, drove him down to the police station, and demanded Chief Wright file the complaint. She was so mad the chief had a hard time understanding her. He called me down to the station to translate. I had to call a rideshare."

All three of them were laughing when the car opened up on the first floor of the courthouse. They made their way through the scanners and metal detectors, collected their purses, and headed to the elevators to the third floor. Even though they were resurrected, Wila wasn't about to make two elderly women climb a couple flights of stairs.

Wila strode into Judge Tellerson's courtroom and stopped in shock. It wasn't her attorney Lilah King talking to the ex-louse's lawyer. Crucifer turned toward Wila and flashed a wide grin.

Chapter 17

Wila couldn't breathe. Gammy, however, charged straight for the demon in the lawyer suit. Thankfully, Crucifer moved away from the opposing attorney before she reached him.

"What do you think you're playing at, boy?" Gammy hissed.

He grabbed her by the arm and led her to Wila.

Gammy jerked free. "Keep your hands off me, or God help me, I'll burn off your dick with holy water."

Crucifer ignored Gammy. "Let's step out of the courtroom, Ms. Ardale." He glanced over his shoulder before he turned back to her. "I don't want to give your ex-husband's lawyer any more ammunition."

At the attention from the other attorney and the bailiff, Wila nodded sharply, though she didn't like the situation one bit. Neither did Sister Joan who had her hand in her purse, no doubt grasping the squirt bottles Father Perez had procured for the resurrected demon hunters. Holy water was the only weapon that could pass through security besides the Soccer Moms' arsenal.

Crucifer led the way to the conference room across the hallway from the courtroom. Once Wila and her party were inside, he closed the door.

"Before you start accusing me of anything, Lilah King had a heart attack before dawn." He rested his briefcase on the table. "She called Chance from the ambulance to cover a child custody hearing for her. War, I did not know this case was about you until I swung by her office to pick up the file."

"Why would she call you?" Wila snapped.

"Lilah was Chance Paxton's mentor when he was fresh out of law school." Crucifer shrugged. "She trusts him."

Wila shot him a nasty smile as she pulled her cell phone out of her jacket pocket. "I'm going to double check." She dialed Lilah's cell phone.

"Hi, Wila," the older woman chirped. "I'm sorry I didn't call you earlier, but I'm in the hospital."

"Are you all right?" Wila could hear voices in the background. They discussed something about EKG readings and blockage.

"I'll be fine" Lilah said nonchalantly. "I asked another attorney, Chance Paxton, to cover your hearing for me. I trained him, so trust me when I say he's good—" Lilah's voice faded with a muffled, "Give me back my phone!"

"Whoever this is, my mother needs surgery—" the new voice said.

"Who are you?" Wila bit back.

"Violet King, and if anything happens to my mother before the surgeon gets her bypass done and the stent in, I'll be the one suing you." The call ended with a click, though Wila got the impression Violet would have slammed the cell phone if she could.

A second later, Lilah texted:

> Sorry about Violet. Chance is an excellent lawyer. I'll call you in a couple of days.

Wila glared at the demon. "I'd better not find out you had anything to do with Lilah's heart attack."

He calmly watched her. "She's an eighty-two-year-old human. I didn't do anything to harm her. I have no reason to harm her."

"Like Gakeel had no reason to ruin Penny's business?" Wila raised her right eyebrow.

He raised his right hand. "I swear by the Silver City in my name and the name of the Prince of Hell I did not hurt Lilah Jane King. I also swear by the above I have not caused you, Wila Latricia Ardale, any harm, I am not causing you any harm, and I will not cause you any harm."

Wila shook her head. "And how am I supposed to believe that?"

He glanced at his watch. "You have a half hour before the judge will start the hearing. You're human. You have free will. It's your choice. If you can find another attorney, I'll step aside. But your son's welfare is at stake, and I do not recommend going into that courtroom without legal representation. You already know your ex-husband and his attorney make me look like an angel."

Wila couldn't stop the chuckles that burbled out of her at his lame joke.

"Are you seriously considering a demon as your lawyer?" Gammy demanded.

"Unless you or Sister Joan can get a law license in the next half hour, I don't see where I have a real choice." Wila looked at her phone screen and began tapping out a text to the Soccer Mom/demon hunter group Francine had set up. "Let me warn my sisters and the incoming demon hunters."

A few seconds after Wila touched the send icon, replies streamed in. As she suspected, Penny and Dani freaked. Francine said Wila didn't have a choice with the short notice, but if she lost custody of Derek, Francine would hold down Crucifer while Wila killed him. Father Perez and the rest of the demon hunters said they would follow the Soccer Moms' lead.

"Well?" Crucifer asked.

Wila looked up from her phone. "Fine. I accept your representation for this hearing. However, you'd better realize you'll die if I lose my son."

The demon released a deep breath. "What if I have to use my powers to get the judge to agree with your side?"

Wila shot him what she knew was an ugly smile. "No demon powers. No demon tricks. If Chance Paxton is as good as Lilah says and you have access to his memories and knowledge, you know how to win this hearing."

The demon rolled his eyes. "Fine. I agree to all your stipulations, War, with one condition. Do I have your assurance that neither the Four Horsemen, your grandmother Latricia Wilkinson, nor anyone living or dead associated in any way, shape, or form with the Catholic Church and/or the

Holy See will do anything to impede me in my representation of you and your son?"

Wila laughed. "You're taking this legal thing literally, aren't you?"

He crossed his arms and watched her. Not even an eyelash moved. She had a female sergeant who used the same technique. When she asked the sergeant about the maneuver's effectiveness, the sergeant smiled and said, "Humans hate silence more than anything."

Now, Wila wondered who taught the sergeant that trick.

She sighed. "All right. I, War, the Third Soccer Mom of the Apocalypse, hereby affirm my sister Soccer Moms, my grandmother Latricia Wilkinson, and no one associated with the Catholic Church will interfere with you, Crucifer, one of the Fallen, Duke of Hell, in the performance of your duties as my substitute legal counsel for the length of this hearing." She made a face at him. "Is that sufficient for you?"

"Yes." For once, the smarmy expression didn't appear on his face. "Now, I have a couple of questions for you about Lilah's notes before we go back into the courtroom."

A shiver ran through Wila. Had she just sold her soul in order to keep her son?

Chapter 18

Apparently, Wila's friends had made their peace with her legal representative being a demon. No one said anything. They all filed in and took seats in the gallery behind Wila. Anyone who'd been a nun, a priest, or a monk in their previous life wore the modern equivalent of their vestments, habits, or robes. Somehow, they managed not to shoot ugly looks at Crucifer, but Penny, Francine, and Dani definitely shot glares at the ex-louse and Rashida.

But worst of all, Courtney Lasser sat behind the ex-louse's party with a smirk on her face.

Part of Wila wanted to look at their souls. But if she discovered the ex-louse's soul was cracked or broken, she didn't know if she could handle what it said about her choice of men.

"All rise," the bailiff called out. "Family Law Court Three-Sixty-Eight is now in session. The Honorable Glenda Tellerson presiding." Everyone stood, though it tickled Wila the ex-louse had to elbow Rashida to get her off her ass.

A wave of sadness wiped away Wila's spiteful humor. She couldn't imagine Rashida as a Soccer Mom in a million years. In the past, she never really questioned why she didn't trust Derek's care with Rashida the way she did with Penny, Francine, or Dani. But the realization her sisters would lay down their lives for her and her son left Wila with a huge knot in her gut that had nothing to do with Rashida's betrayal, and everything to do with Wila's misjudgment of her ex-friend's character.

She prayed she wasn't making the same mistake by trusting Crucifer.

Judge Tellerson entered from the back door of the courtroom. A pearl chain draped from her tortoise-shell glasses and around her neck. A fluffy sheer bow decorated the throat of her robes. And her hair was pulled in such a tight bun the judge didn't need Botox.

"Be seated." She frowned at the ex-louse's attorney. "Why the hell is this case before me again, Mr. Hannity?"

He cleared his throat. "There's been a material change to the living conditions of my client's son."

The judge's attention shifted to the ex-louse. "Mr. Jackson, you got divorced five years ago. You remarried. Your former wife is allowed to date. I am not in the mood for petty bullshit today."

"This isn't a matter of someone Ms. Ardale may be seeing socially." Hannity cleared his throat again. "First of all, she has a dead person living with her. Specifically, Latricia K. Wilkinson who passed away eleven years ago. A copy of her death certificate is attached to the motion, Your Honor."

The court clerk handed Judge Tellerson the file.

She flipped through the paperwork before she looked at Hannity again. "And?"

"She-she's dead," Hannity protested.

"Mr. Hannity, in case you haven't noticed, nearly half of the deceased in the county have risen from their graves over the past three weeks." She folded her hands, probably to keep from strangling the attorney. "In fact, Mayor Oldham initiated a program asking citizens to help temporarily house the dead because winter is coming. Furthermore, there is no allegations in your motion where Ms. Wilkinson has endangered your client's minor son."

"That's Mrs. Wilkinson."

At Gammy's voice, Wila dug her nails into her palms.

"Excuse me?" The judge peered over the rims of her glasses at the gallery behind Wila.

Crucifer stood. "What my client's grandmother meant is she was happily married in her life, and she prefers to be addressed by her traditional title of Mrs. Wilkinson. We apologize for the interruption." He shot a look at Hannity before he resumed his seat.

Wila turned toward Gammy and motioned for her to sit. Gammy gave Wila what she and her cousins referred to as the evil eye, but Gammy resumed her seat between Sister Joan and Laura Hudson. Penny's mother-in-law whispered in Gammy's ear, and Gammy nodded.

"I apologize for interrupting, Your Honor," Gammy said.

"Thank you, Mrs. Wilkinson." Judge Tellerson smiled at her. The judge never smiled in court according to Lilah, but the lady on the bench was one hundred percent live human. "And I apologize for using the wrong title."

The judge turned back to Hannity. "Well, counselor? Is your only objection due to Mrs. Wilkinson's status as a resurrected person?"

"My client's child support is being used to feed and clothe Mrs. Wilkinson," he tried to take a different tactic.

Wila could literally feel Gammy's anger build, and the emotion fed her alter ego's power. She stared at her lap and recited a Buddhist mantra to keep War under control. God only knew what would happen if her eyes turned red in front of the judge and the ex-louse's lawyer.

The judge glanced at the paperwork. "Anything else?"

"Your Honor, living with a dead person cannot be healthy for any child," Hannity said. "There's no precedent for this type of situation. Then, there is the fact that Ms. Ardale was recorded on video threatening a Mrs. Courtney Lasser at the Oakfield Recreational Park Tuesday evening. My client is rightly concerned about the environment his son is living in."

The judge pursed her lips at the last statement. Wila's whole body went numb. This was so not good. She looked like a crazy person on that video.

Especially with Brian hanging onto her to keep her from grabbing Courtney's phone out of her manicured claws.

"Is that what is on the video file you submitted?"

"Yes, Your Honor."

Judge Tellerson tapped the tablet sitting on her desk. Wila winced at her own voice shrieking from the device's speakers. But instead of anger or derision, the judge looked confused.

"Mr. Paxton, did you know you were on this video?"

Crucifer stood. "I was discussing a separate business opportunity with Ms. Ardale and her associates. I learned about the recording earlier today when Ms. King asked me to cover this hearing."

"Speaking of which, where is Ms. King this morning? It's not like her to miss a court appearance."

"She had a heart attack, Your Honor," he stated. "To the best of my knowledge, she's in surgery right now."

The judge leaned back in her chair. "Lilah had a heart attack?"

"Yes, ma'am."

"So you didn't see Ms. Lasser recording your talk with Ms. Ardale?"

"No, Your Honor."

"Is there anything you want to strike as privileged before I admit this into the record?"

"Actually, Your Honor, I'd like the whole video stricken from the record. The evidence is irrelevant to this proceeding."

Wila crossed her fingers under the table.

Hannity jumped to his feet. "This video goes to show Ms. Ardale's lack of fitness to care for her son!"

The judge regarded him for a long moment before she said, "I'll hold my ruling on the evidence objection until the end of the hearing. Anything further, Mr. Hannity?"

"No, Your Honor." He sat, a sour look on his face. Deion whispered furiously in Hannity's ear. Her ex probably believed the video was the nail to get full physical custody of Derek.

Wila swallowed the lump in her throat. The judge could just as easily rule against her after that performance at the soccer field.

"Mr. Paxton, you made proceed," the judge said.

Wila looked up at him.

"Your Honor, since both my client and her grandmother's integrity are being questioned, I'd like their testimony on the record," he said.

"Very well." The judge leaned back in her seat while the ex-louse made more angry hissing noises in his own attorney's ear.

The demon turned to Gammy. "Mrs. Wilkinson, would you please take the witness stand?"

She stood with her chin raised and marched up to the little boxed area next to the judge's bench.

Once the judge swore in Gammy, she said, "You may proceed, counselor."

Crucifer stepped to the front of the attorney table. "Mrs. Wilkinson, would you please state your full name for the record?"

"Latricia Kande Wilkinson."

"What is your relationship to Derek Jackson?"

"He's my great-grandson."

"Why are you living with Ms. Ardale and Derek?"

Gammy swallowed hard. "I didn't have any place else to go after I climbed out of my grave. I sold my house in Chicago to one of my grand-sons, and the apartment I was living in here in Oakfield before I died had been rented out to someone else."

"Do you pay Ms. Ardale for staying in her house?"

"Not yet." Gammy glared at the ex-louse. "I just started working at Java's Palace yesterday, and I haven't received my first paycheck yet. However, I intend to repay my granddaughter and her friends for housing, feeding, and clothing me for the last three weeks. After that, I'll see about taking care of myself for however long the Good Lord decides I should stay on this earth for the second time."

"Have you ever harmed Derek?"

"Heavens, no!"

"Has Ms. Ardale ever harmed Derek?"

Gammy shook her head emphatically. "Never!"

Crucifer gestured toward the ex-louse. "Has Mr. Jackson ever harmed Derek?"

"Yes."

Deion leapt to his feet. "That was an accident!"

"Your baby was screaming bloody murder, and you didn't think to check the temperature of the bath water!" Gammy shot back.

The judge banged her gavel. "That's enough! Mr. Hannity, get your client under control. Mr. Paxton, the same goes for your witness. Otherwise, I'll hold all of you in contempt."

All of Wila's attempts at self-control faded. Deion had claimed Gammy burned Derek with the too-hot bath. She rose to her feet, her flaming sword in her right hand. "You hurt our son and blamed my grandmother for what you did?" she growled. "You bastard."

And for the first time ever, Deion didn't look so damn confident.

Chapter 19

Rashida screamed. Boney hands dug into Wila's shoulders and slammed her back into her chair.

"Get control of yourself. This is a court of human law, not the plain of Armageddon," Dani's voice rattled.

Wila looked over her left shoulder. Green light from Dani's eye sockets bored into Wila. Her own anger had triggered her sisters' transformations, too. Oh, God! She'd royally screwed up. Father Perez and all the demon hunters sat quietly, waiting for an indication from the Soccer Moms of what to do.

And for once, none of this was a demon's fault.

"Well, I'll be damned," Judge Tellerson murmured. "The rumors are true. I thought the videos had been doctored." She turned to her bailiff. "Deputy Carson, did you know about Ms. Ardale?"

The bailiff stood and rested his hands on his belt. "Famine and several of the demon hunters present have been training both the sheriff and police departments. With the manifestation of the Four Horsemen here in Oak-field, we've had a rise in citizens possessed by demons over the last month and a half. I'm sorry, but everything was supposed to be on a need-to-know basis, Your Honor."

Judge Tellerson removed her glasses and pinched the bridge of her nose for a long moment. Wila looked at Crucifer. He shrugged.

Damn, she'd technically broke her deal with the demon by ruining his chances of winning the hearing the human way. Her heart thudded in her chest. If she lost custody of Derek, it was her own damn fault.

The judge finally replaced her glasses. "Mr. Paxton, were there any further questions for Mrs. Wilkinson?"

"No, Your Honor."

"Mr. Hannity, any questions for this witness?"

The ex-louse's attorney rose with a nervous glance at Wila before he turned his attention to Gammy. "Mrs. Wilkinson, did my client purposely hurt his son?"

"I can't answer to his intentions, sir," Gammy said coolly.

"Isn't it possible my client used water that was too hot through inexperience in child care because this was his first child?"

"It's possible," Gammy grudgingly admitted. "But Derek isn't his first child. Just the first one he's taken responsibility for."

Wila's throat went dry. Deion had kids before she met him? She wasn't sure why, but that knowledge made her heart ache though it didn't really surprise her. Not after everything he pulled over the years.

"No further questions for the witness." Hannity sat stiffly in his seat, obviously not happy about being surprised in court.

"You may step down, Mrs. Wilkinson," Judge Tellerson said.

Gammy crossed the floor and resumed her seat on the bench behind Wila. At the other table, the ex-louse and his attorney hissed at each other obviously looking for a way to redeem their complaint against Gammy living with Wila.

Unfortunately, Wila had just handed them everything they needed on the proverbial silver platter.

Crucifer stood again. "I'd like to call Ms. Wila Ardale to the stand."

Panicked, she looked up at him, but he gave her an encouraging nod and mouthed, "Trust me."

Wila rose and stiffly crossed to the witness stand. She couldn't relax enough to get rid of her fatigues or weapon.

"Could you sheath the flaming sword, Ms. Ardale?" the judge requested dryly. "You're making my bailiff nervous."

Sure enough, the deputy was on his feet, his hand on his taser.

"Oh, sorry." Wila reached over her shoulder and slid the sword into its sheath attached to her rucksack. "I apologize, ma'am. That's the best I can do right now."

"That's acceptable to me," the judge said. "Is it acceptable to you, Deputy Carson?"

"As long as she doesn't reach for that sword while she's in the courtroom, I won't shock her." The bailiff sat back down, but from the look on his face, tasing her wasn't an idle threat.

Judge Tellerson swore Wila in before she nodded to Crucifer. "You may proceed, Mr. Paxton."

"Would you please state your name for the record?" he said.

"Wila Latricia Ardale."

"And what is your title?"

She didn't like making this official through the court record, but she was the one who lost control in front of the judge and the ex-louse. "I am War, the Third Soccer Mom of the Apocalypse."

"Whoa," the judge interrupted. "What do you mean by Soccer Mom of the Apocalypse?"

"None of us are men, all of our kids play on the same youth soccer team, and we all drive minivans." Wila shrugged. "Calling ourselves the Four Horsemen didn't sound right."

The corners of the judge's lips quirked. She glanced at Penny, Francine, and Dani sitting together behind Crucifer before the judge said, "Continue."

"Ms. Ardale, have you ever harmed your son Derek?"

"No."

"Has your grandmother Mrs. Wilkinson ever harmed your son?

"No."

"Ms. Ardale, what security precautions did you take at your home before the Apocalypse started?" Crucifer said.

Now, where was he going with this? Yeah, she broke their agreement, but he had asked her to trust him after she blew up in the courtroom. It was too late to stop now. Not if she wanted to keep Derek.

"I had a professional system installed at the house I own when Derek and I moved in. It has sensors on all the doors and windows. I recently bought motion sensors, cameras, and extra security lights for the exterior, but my plans to install them this morning had to be delayed."

"Since the beginning of the Apocalypse, what extra security precautions have you enacted?"

"Both my grandmother and my son have their own bodyguards when I'm not with them."

"Are those bodyguards present today?"

"My grandmother's bodyguard is present in court." Wila had to swallow a smile as she realized Crucifer's tactic. "Derek's bodyguard is at his school."

"Why do you have bodyguards for your household members?"

"Demons kidnapped Pestilence's daughter by possessing the girl's father. All of the immediate family members of the Soccer Moms are guarded by professional demon hunters who are risen dead."

"Why specifically do you use the resurrected demon hunters?"

"Because they cannot be possessed by demons."

Crucible turned to Hannity. "Your witness." The demon sat, but he didn't have the usual self-satisfied smirk. He played the serious attorney seeking to protect his client and her family very well.

The ex-louse whispered in his attorney's ear. Hannity nodded before he stood and moved in front of his table, but from the stink of fear rolling of him, he wouldn't come any closer to Wila or her sisters.

"Ms. Ardale, why didn't you tell Mr. Jackson his son was in danger?"

"Because as Deputy Carson said, knowledge about the Soccer Moms and the demon hunters were treated as need to know."

"So, you left my client and his wife in danger of possession rather than tell him the truth about yourself?"

"The only way Mr. Jackson would be in any danger of possession while Derek wasn't with him is if I still loved him," she said sadly. "Or if I were still friends with Mrs. Jackson. Since neither situation exists, there is a very low chance of them being possessed. I'm more concerned about Derek's teachers being possessed."

"Ms. Ardale, you testified the only people who can't be possessed are the people recently resurrected." Glee sparkled in Hannity's eyes.

She smiled. "My apologies for not being clear earlier. Demons can't possess any dead person, resurrected or not."

Hannity rested his ass against his table. "Do you love your son Derek?"

"Yes."

"And how do you prevent him from being possessed?" Saccharine coated is voice. He wanted her to lose control again.

Wila took a deep breath. "Show tunes."

"I beg your pardon?" That was obviously not the answer he was expecting.

"It's how the Soccer Moms keep demons out." She shrugged. "Sitcom theme songs and children's ditties like 'Baby Shark' work, too."

"Is that the reason every radio station has been playing obnoxiously happy pop tunes or Christmas songs the last couple of weeks?" Judge Tellerson asked.

Wila looked up at her. "Yes, Your Honor. The Red Cross had Broadway songs playing at the shelters during the days, but they turned off the music one night at the high school so folks could sleep, and . . . things went south."

The judge frowned. "That was the reason for the so-called riot at the school a couple of days before Halloween?"

"I'm afraid so."

"I object, Your Honor!" Hannity straightened. "You've inserted yourself in the middle of my cross-examination of the witness!"

She stared at him through narrowed eyes. "Then please continue, counselor."

He opened his mouth, then closed it. After a moment, he sheepishly said, "Nothing further, Your Honor."

The judge glanced at Wila. "You may step down, Ms. Ardale. Any further witnesses, Mr. Paxton?"

As Wila crossed back to her chair, she realized her black suit had replaced her fatigues. The rest of her sisters looked normal again as well.

Crucifer stood to address Judge Tellerson while Wila resumed her seat beside him. "My remaining witnesses would be telling the court the same thing from their individual perspectives regarding the protection of the blood relatives of the Soccer Moms of the Apocalypse, including Derek Jackson. It would be repetitious, but if the court or opposing counsel wishes me to be thorough . . ."

Hannity glared at the demon before he turned back to the judge. "That won't be necessary, Your Honor. I'll stipulate to opposing counsel's testimony of any further witnesses."

"Anything further, Mr. Hannity?" she asked.

"No, ma'am."

From the nasty look the ex-louse gave his own attorney, he probably wished he'd represented himself and saved the money. Wila bit her bottom lip to keep from laughing out loud.

The judge's nostrils flared, and lines marred her forehead. "The claims and testimony of both parties put the court in a bit of a pickle. Mr. Jackson asserted the minor child Derek Jackson in this case is in danger. And he's correct. Derek is in danger—by living with Mr. Jackson during the current world circumstances."

Wila's chest ached, and she clenched her fists. Was Judge Tellerson going to take Derek away from both her and the ex-louse? He'd be placed in a foster home.

And totally at the mercy of any random demon.

"And given those circumstances, I am temporarily amending the custody orders regarding Derek Jackson. Wila Ardale will have full physical custody at all times from now until either we all go to Heaven or the Soccer Moms of the Apocalypse find a way to stop the end of the world."

The ex-louse ruined Wila's momentary relief by leaping to his feet. "You can't do this! I haven't done anything wrong!"

"Take it up on appeal," Judge Tellerson said. "Mr. Paxton, Mr. Hannity, my clerk will bring you certified copies of my ruling in a few minutes. Court is dismissed." She rose from her chair and marched out of the courtroom.

The ex-louse turned to Wila. "You'll pay for this, you bitch!"

Crucifer stalked over to opposing counsel's table. When he spoke, his voice held a deadly edge. "Mr. Jackson, you were the fool who choose to cause trouble for your ex-wife out of spite. The truly sad part is through your spite, you and your wife lost the protection of the Vatican taskforce."

"This ruling isn't going to hold up, Chance," Hannity said. "And you know it."

"It will hold up long enough." Crucifer flashed him a nasty smile.

Wila wasn't sure what to say or do. The only people who stood up for her had been Gammy, and now, the other Soccer Moms. For a demon to do so was-was . . .

"Ms. Ardale." Crucifer held open the little swinging gate between the spectator benches and the rest of the courtroom.

She looked behind her and realized only her sisters, Laura Hudson, and Gammy remained. Forcing herself to her feet, she stalked out of the courtroom. The rest of the women on her side and her demon attorney followed.

As they waited for the elevator, Wila eyed Crucifer. "I don't suppose you handle tort cases, do you?"

"Are you asking me to represent you in another case?" Still no smarmy look on his face. Nope, his expression was definitely surprise.

"Yeah." She nodded. "Despite my screw-up in the courtroom, you stuck to your end of the bargain."

He inclined his head. "I would be pleased to represent you in another legal matter, Ms. Ardale."

Wila ignored Gammy's scowl. Maybe Crucifer was serious about helping the Soccer Moms stop the Apocalypse after all.

Chapter 20

Wila texted Derek on the ride down the elevator, telling him not to leave with anyone other than her after school. She asked the demon hunter Karen Longstreet to give Gammy and Sister Joan a ride home while the Soccer Moms retreated to Java's Palace. They needed to discuss the ramifications of taking Crucifer up on his offer to help them stop the Apocalypse in return for the throne of Hell.

And they needed to discuss the matter without input from Gammy and the demon hunters.

Java's Palace was pretty empty for a Thursday afternoon. Since Francine's order was done first, she grabbed the booth where the Soccer Moms normally sat.

Wila glanced out the window facing Baxter Street as she strode back to their Soccer Moms' meeting area. Of course, Crucifer sat inside Chance Paxton's expensive, sporty sedan in the parking lot and watched the coffee shop. Could he exhibit any more desperation?

She slid into the booth next to Francine. "Thanks for backing me up today."

Francine smiled. "We all did."

"You're the only one who didn't call me crazy for letting a demon represent me in court after Lilah had her heart attack."

"I just hope she's all right," Francine murmured.

"They were getting ready to wheel her into surgery when I spoke with her this morning." Wila sighed. "Her daughter also threatened to sue me."

"Don't take it personally." Francine laid her right hand over Wila's left one and squeezed. "If my mother's clients called her while she was in the ER, I'd be snappish, too."

"Why are you two holding hands?" Penny said as she sat on the opposing bench. She slid over so Dani could sit beside her.

"Maybe we kissed and made up," Wila bit back. "Can we discuss real problems please? Like the pathetic demon sitting in your parking lot?"

Francine released Wila's hand. "I'm concerned about how much support he can garner in Hell. We may be able to put him on the throne, but that doesn't mean he can hold it."

"Yeah, what if he expects us to become the new Dukes of Hell?" Worry scrunched Dani's face. "As depressing as my life is, I don't want to give it up."

Penny shrugged. "Then we make sure the limitations of our participation are in the contract."

"Wait a minute." Wila waved her hands. "Dani, are you admitting your life is depressing?"

"All right." Dani took a shuddering breath. "I'm scared. I'm worried we will be sucked into something we can't handle. Or we've gone too far and it's already too late. I'm sorry, Wila, but at least, Derek does have his father in his life. What if I screw up and make Mark an orphan?"

"Then let's make a deal," Wila said. "If we stop the Apocalypse and survive doing so, you will accept a date with Ramon. Just one date. It's been almost seven years, sweetie. It's time to get back on the horse, and I don't mean Verde."

Dani cocked her head. "I have to date? What about you? You've been divorced almost as long as I've been widowed. If I agree to going out with Ramon, it will be a double-date with you and your suitor."

"I don't have a suitor." Wila scowled at Dani.

"You've got someone shooting for the job." Francine sipped her coffee.

Wila groaned. "Would you please let that go?"

"No, wait," Penny said. "Francine may be gross and disgusting, but maybe there is something to Crucifer's obsession with you other than her crappy attempts at matchmaking."

"Excuse me?" Francine narrowed her eyes.

"What if Chance Paxton's soul is having an affect on Broccoli?" Excitement gleamed in Penny's eyes. "What if he's been in Hell since the Fall? As a former angel, he may have the raw power to possess someone, but maybe not the experience with human emotions."

"Where is this coming from?" Wila blurted. "He may have been an angel once upon a time, but now, he's pure demon."

Penny cocked her head. "Have you noticed you've been calling Kale 'him' for the past couple of days?"

"He's—" Wila started.

All three of her friends smirked.

"Chance Paxton is a man," Wila growled. "Excuse me for not getting the pronouns for all the entities in Paxton's body correct."

"Actually, that's my point," Penny said. "Cabbage's attitude, especially toward you, has really changed over the past three days. He's gone from making raunchy comments to get under your skin to being your knight in shining armor in court."

"I don't know." Wila shook her head. "I think you're reaching to come up with a motivation. And might I point out you just used male pronouns for the demon watching us from his car?"

"Wila's right," Dani said. "This attitude shift could be a manipulative demon game."

"Or maybe Penny's right, and Chance Paxton's emotions are affecting Brussel Sprout," Francine countered. "If Cauliflower wasn't riding Chance, and Lilah had introduced you to him properly, would you have accepted an offer to talk over coffee with him?"

Wila turned to Penny. "This is another reason you need to keep Java's Palace open later. Francine needs coffee dates."

"It also means Francine's right." Dani smirked. "You find Chance Paxton attractive."

"What you all are leaving out is I haven't met the real Chance yet," Wila protested. "What if you're right, and Crucifer's change in behavior is a con job on a lonely, single mom?"

Francine snorted coffee out her nose.

"We can argue about his motivations and Chance's effect on the demon until the end of the world," Penny said once Francine could breathe without coughing. "But it doesn't solve our immediate problem. Do we take Broccoli up on his offer?" Leave it to her to cut through the bull.

"What if we add in a few stipulations?" Wila said.

"Like what?" Dani said.

Wila grinned. "We could use him to find out what Pence, Courtney, and the ex-louse are plotting."

Francine pulled a notebook and pen from her tote. "Let's make a list of what we want. If he wants our help, we need it to be worth our while."

An hour and another round of coffees later, the Soccer Moms had their list of conditions for the demon. Dani stalked out to Paxton's silver sports car and invited him into Java's Palace for their discussion.

Once he was seated in an extra chair at the head of their booth, Penny laid out their first requirement.

Crucifer stared at her with an aghast expression. "Do you have any idea of what you're asking? Even by demon standards, Pence is gross as fuck!"

"Keep your voice down," Wila snapped. She looked around, but the handful of other patrons who sat in the dining area merely glanced at them before resuming their own conversations. "The other option is you possess my former husband. And if you do that, I doubt you'll want to give up his harem."

"This seems terribly unprofessional, War, ur, Ms. Ardale." Crucifer pursed his mouth. "This sounds like petty human revenge bullshit on the ex."

"We need to know what information Pence, Courtney, and the ex-louse shared about us," Dani said.

"We've got humans coming after us because we are the Soccer Moms of the Apocalypse," Francine added.

"And Pence has been at the center of a lot of human-related problems. We can't help you with your plan until we get these losers off our backs," Penny finished.

Crucible shook his head. "Gakeel and his nest were idiots for taking you ladies head on."

"What does that have to do with Pence?" Dani demanded.

"They drew too much attention from other humans," the demon said with total disgust in his voice.

"True." Wila crossed her arms. "The other question we have is whether you can keep control of Hell after you take over."

"The only one I can't destroy by myself is the Morningstar." He grinned. "Which is why I need you ladies."

"As long as you understand we don't serve you," Wila shot back. "You keep the throne on your own and your demons in check. You or any other demon comes back to earth—"

"I'm a shish kebab." He rolled his eyes. "I got it. Are you sure you can trust the Kid and the Catholic Church?"

"What's that supposed to mean?" Dani snapped.

He frowned. "They traditionally don't like women in power."

"Neither does Hell," Penny said dryly. "What's your point?"

"The demons and the humans aren't the only ones keeping tabs on you." Crucifer shrugged. "But like the Kid says you have free will. That doesn't mean both sides can't manipulate you."

"Like you can?" Wila bit out.

He shrugged again. "Even if I do this little spy mission for you, you have no way of knowing whether my report is true."

"That's the reason we'll do some double-checking of our own," Francine said coolly.

He pushed to his feet. "Fine. I agree to your terms, ladies. I'll get back to you once I've learned the information you desire." He replaced the chair to its position at the closest table and stalked out of the coffee shop.

As Wila watched him leave, a disturbing thought occurred to her. What if she was really attracted to Crucible no matter who he wore?

Chapter 21

That very question started Wila's hands shaking. Her heart raced. No, she'd kept it together for this long. She was not about to have an anxiety attack in public. Especially not in the middle of her sister's café.

And not over a stupid demon.

"I need to go pick up Derek. Catch you guys later." She slid out of the booth and raced for the door.

Once outside, she climbed into Scarlett and locked the minivan doors before she leaned her forehead against the steering wheel and tried to calm her heart through one of the breathing techniques her therapist had taught her.

The radio flared to life. "Are you—are you-you-you—all right? Did the—demon—cause you grief?"

"This isn't about the demon," Wila lied.

"Pants—fire sale," Scarlett responded.

Wila gulped air. Thankfully, her minivan/horse remained silent.

The lock on the front passenger door popped, and a blast of chilly wind hit Wila. Her head jerked up as Francine climbed inside and slammed the door shut.

"Take it easy on me," Scarlett sang.

"Not to mention, that's a good way to get yourself shish kebab'd," Wila said sourly. "And how did you get inside my girl?"

"I asked Scarlett nicely." Francine replied. "And I apologize for slamming your door, Scarlett. I'll be more careful in the future."

"I couldn't—let her cry," Scarlett wailed.

"You haven't had a panic attack like that for a while," Francine added.

"What do you know about them?" Wila glared at her.

"I used to get them." Francine grimaced. "It's part of why my mom pushed me into pageants and cheerleading. She thought public appearances and speaking would help me get over my attacks."

"Did it?"

"Anti-anxiety medication was a bigger help." Francine chuckled.

Wila leaned back against her seat. "I didn't want drugs. That's why my therapist suggestion meditation and yoga."

"I wasn't judging. Whatever helps you keep your head on straight."

"Is that the reason for your aloof superiority? You don't want people to see your weakness?"

"Actually, it was learning not to care about what other people think." A self-deprecating chuckle burst from Francine. "It just took me longer than I realized."

"I apologize for ever thinking you were a Karen," Wila murmured.

"I admit sometimes I do wear the Karen armor." Francine eyed her. "Please don't ever tell a certain demon hunter who is living at my house I said that."

"I won't." Wila smiled. "Her stabby weapons would actually hurt you." She feared the answer to her next question, but she needed to know. "Do Penny and Dani know?"

"Yeah, we've all had similar problems so we recognize the symptoms." Francine shrugged. "But since you never brought it up, none of us said anything. Penny was sure you'd tell us when you were ready."

Wila's eyes burned, and she stared out the windshield, willing herself not to cry. "I—" She coughed to clear the lump at the back of her throat. "I didn't have any room to talk. Not when Penny didn't know if Justine would survive. Not when Dani lost her husband."

"You're not the only vet who didn't have a chance to process what happened in Afghanistan until you got home. That kind of crap—"

"It's not just my service." Wila closed her eyes and sucked in a deep breath. "My mom and my brother were killed in a drive-by."

When Francine remained silent, the words poured out of Wila. "I was with them. Watende shielded me with his own body. Dad's grief consumed him, and—" She looked at Francine. "In the beginning, I didn't like you because you reminded me too much of Mom. You and Brittany remind me of how we used to be."

"Would you mind terribly if I took that as a compliment?" Francine smiled.

"No, I guess not."

"Is that when you went to live with your grandmother?"

Wila nodded.

"Do you want to talk to her?"

"No." A weak chuckle followed. "She's heard all this before."

"You okay to drive?" Francine asked. "If not, Scarlett can take you home, and I'll pick up Derek from school for you."

"Thanks, but no." Wila sighed. "I texted him to only come home with me in case the ex-louse does something really, really stupid this afternoon."

"He was pretty pissed after the judge's ruling," Francine agreed. "If you're sure . . ."

"I'm sure." Wila smiled. "Thank you though."

"That's what sisters are for."

Once Wila assured Francine she was all right, again, and Francine climbed out of Scarlett, Wila headed for the school to pick up Derek. It was stupid to go this early and wait in the pickup line, but she needed a little time to herself.

And she wasn't about to get it at home. Not with Gammy and Sister Joan trying to take care of her.

Unfortunately, Courtney Lasser was already parked at the beginning of the pickup line. A stream of invectives ran through Wila's brain, none of them fit for polite company. She was wrong. Not every Karen was a blond, but this one did have highlights.

And Wila would love to rip out every lock of Courtney's perfectly coiffed chestnut locks tinged with caramel.

"I could—big butt—the bitch," Scarlett said.

"You are not rear-ending her minivan," Wila snapped. Thankfully, Scarlett didn't assert control over herself. Wila braked to a stop behind the gold minivan and turned off the engine.

"I'm sorry, baby," she added. "The last thing I want is for you to hurt yourself over that woman. And please don't call her a bitch in front of Gammy or Derek. I know my language went downhill while in the Army, but I'm trying to be better for their sakes."

"You are—simply the best," Scarlett sang.

Wila chuckled and patted the dashboard. "You are, too."

"Danger! Danger! Red Alert!" Scarlett cried.

Wila looked up in time to see Courtney slam her driver side door shut and approached Scarlett, wearing a familiar smirk.

Except it wasn't only Courtney inside her body.

What the hell was Crucifer up to now?

Chapter 22

Wila tapped the control to lower her door window. "What do you think you're doing, Bok Choy?"

His smirk faded. "You know, War, the cruciferous vegetable jokes from you ladies are getting old."

"You're possessing a woman who sued me yesterday," Wila snapped. "The same one who tried to help my ex-husband take my son from me. Forgive me if I don't feel like playing nice."

"She really doesn't like you either." He gestured at the passenger side. "Mind if we talk in some warmth?"

"You okay with this, Scarlett?" Wila asked.

"No—but—I'll— do it."

Crucible circled around Scarlett while Wila rolled up her window and unlocked the passenger side door. He, or rather she, climbed into the seat and gently shut the door. Wila turned on the engine to warm up the cabin.

"Thank you for your hospitality—" He sang a few notes that were a cross between robins and how she imagined angels sounded like. "And thank you, too, War."

"My name is—Scarlett!" her horse yelled through the speakers.

"What were you stupid enough to call her?"

Crucifer actually looked confused. "Her name. There's no perfect translation into your language."

Wila pursed her lips for a moment. "Try me."

"Roughly, her name is The Vehicle of Conflict."

"That's a description of her role in the Apocalypse." Wila stared at the soccer youth league sticker on the rear window of Courtney's minivan. "That's not a name."

"So where does the name Scarlett come from?"

Wila grinned and looked at Crucifer. "Scarlett O'Hara from *Gone with the Wind*."

He rolled his eyes. "You humans are so weird."

"I thought the plan was to possess Pence. Why the hell are you in Courtney?"

"I wanted to know if she approached your ex-husband or if he approached her."

"And?"

"Lasser went to Jackson because she believed he would be more inclined to take on her civil case against you because of your bitter divorce. She knew nothing about you in particular being a Soccer Mom of the Apocalypse until you revealed yourself to her two nights ago. She showed him the film."

His mouth twisted before he added, "Given you and your sisters are rebelling against Lasser's authority as president of the Oakfield Parents Association, why don't you have any sympathy for our position?"

"Your position?" She raised her eyebrows. "You mean the Fallen and the rest of the demons?"

"Yes."

"You are comparing the woman you are possessing with God?"

"Yes."

"Have you lost your ever-loving mind?"

"You think you're better than me?" he taunted.

"Which you?"

He shot her a Courtney sneer. "Me as in Crucifer."

"No." Wila sighed. "I get having father issues."

"So, you think you're better than Courtney Lasser?"

Wila made a circular motion with her index finger. "Will she remember any of this?"

From his expression, he was thoroughly insulted. "None of the humans who've served me remember anything. I'm a duke of Hell, not one of the hoi polloi demons like Gakeel."

"Sounds like Courtney's bad manners are affecting you, Broccoli," Wila mocked. "You might not want to stay in there too long."

Crucifer shook his borrowed head. "I'm fully aware of her emotions. I thought Pence was full of hate, but Lasser takes it to a new level."

"I thought you could only possess people who are hopeless, in pain, or full of fear," Wila commented.

"Where do you think Pence and Lasser's hatred comes from?"

"I don't understand."

"Not everyone turns their pain on themselves or tries to heal themselves like you."

Wila's blood turned to ice in her veins. "What's that supposed to mean?"

"Never mind."

What all did he know about her? Maybe he was being a manipulative jerk. It wouldn't be that hard to simply google her name and discover a ton about her. Fine then. She wouldn't take his bait.

Crucifer blew out a deep breath. "Tell your sisters I'll meet all of you at your home at eight tonight. And I will be riding Pence, so please don't do anything stupid when I come to your door."

"Like having one of the priest bless the sprinklers and turning them on when you arrive?" She shot him a vicious grin.

"You haven't cleared your lines for the winter yet?" He clicked his tongue. "You're going to ruin your pipes that way."

"How would you know about sprinkler systems?" she asked.

He shrugged. "I know a lot of things. Especially about plumbing."

And the smarmy behavior was back.

Wila cocked her head as she regarded him. "You do realize you're in

Courtney Lasser's body when you say that? You know, the woman who hates me and has sued me?"

"We could make a sex tape of the two of you together." A sly grin crossed his face. "That would really tick her off."

She shuddered. "Ewwww. No. Absolutely not. That's worse than the thought of Pence on my doorstep."

"Well, a sex tape of you and him—"

"Shut up, Bok Choy," she said, but there was no real bite to her words. "And get out of my minivan before she decides to trample you to death."

"See you later, War." Crucifer opened the passenger door and exited.

Wila watched him return to Courtney's vehicle and climb inside.

Unfortunately, her question from the coffee shop had been answered. God help her, she was attracted to a duke of Hell.

Chapter 23

The school's bells rang, and kids poured through the doors. Derek ran up to Scarlett, opened the door, and leapt inside.

"Dad lost, huh?" He wore an impish grin while he buckled his seatbelt.

"You knew about the emergency hearing?"

Derek rolled his eyes. "Dad didn't want me to know, but Rashida spilled the beans. They both were freaked about Gammy being alive. And then, Kenny's mom sent him the video of you going all War after the game on Tuesday."

Wila winced as she pulled away from the curb. "You saw the video?"

"Yeah, Dad made a point of showing it to me and trying to get information about you from me." He sighed. "Mom, you did the right thing by leaving Dad. He and Rashida have turned into such drama queens."

Wila bit her lower lip to keep from saying anything bad about the ex-louse and her former best friend. Gammy was right. Deion was still Derek's father.

"Don't worry," Derek continued. "I didn't tell them anything. In fact, I may have suggested Kenny's mom made him add special effects to the video."

Wila couldn't stop her snort of laughter. "I'm sorry they laid all of that on you. It should have stayed between the adults. But I don't want you lying to your father either."

"Mom, we're talking about the end of the world."

She didn't like how terribly mature her son sounded.

"There's more important things going on besides Dad and Rashida's petty bullshit," he continued.

"Derek!"

"He-he-he's—right, you know," Scarlett added.

"I'm sorry for swearing," Derek murmured. "I promise not to do it in front of Gammy and Sister Joan, but you've got to admit Dad's crap is petty." And the way he accepted Scarlett talking through the radio meant her steed had talked to her son privately long before now.

Wila sighed. "You'll get no argument from me there."

"Now, I've got a question for you."

She could feel Derek's gaze boring through her skull. "Okay. What is it?"

"Why aren't you at work?"

"Captain Miller gave me the day off for the hearing."

"Have you told him about your side hustle?"

"My side hustle?" Wila glanced at her son, but he was being totally serious.

"Being a Soccer Mom," Derek elaborated.

"He . . . already knew, but he call me into his office on Monday to admit it to me. He added if I needed time-off for apocalyptic stuff to give him a call and he'd make sure my shift was covered."

"He's a cool boss."

Wila smiled. "Yes, he is."

She considered her next words carefully. "Speaking of Tuesday night, what was that kiss from Brittany about?"

"It was nothing," he muttered.

"Do you like her? Because she seems to like you."

"Mom, stay out of it."

"All right, but just do me a favor," she said. "Please don't go to Mark, his uncle, or his grandfather for advice about girls."

"That leaves only Doctor Gene because I sure can't ask Brittany's dad or Justine's grandpa." Derek chortled. "And if my dad knew what he was doing, you guys wouldn't have gotten a divorce."

Wila couldn't help it. She laughed out loud with her son. In a way, she was relieved that Derek had a plan in place. And for all of Gene's peccadillos, he would do his best to steer Derek appropriately.

"How does Burrito Barn sound for dinner?" she asked once their mirth died.

"You getting tired of Gammy's ham and greens, too?"

"Don't you ever tell her because I do love her cooking, but three nights in a row is a bit too much, even for me."

"Gammy made you and the other moms eat leftovers last night?"

"She tried." Wila grinned. "That's the reason there's still some leftover."

The two of them laughed the rest of the way home.

This time, no one's car was waiting in the Ardale driveway when Wila pulled into the garage. In the kitchen, she found Gammy and Sister Joan sitting at the kitchen table, their heads bent over Wila's laptop.

"Please tell me you two haven't discovered internet porn." Wila sat her purse on the counter and scratched both Martin and Malcom's chins in greeting.

"Ewww! Mom!" Derek protested as he headed straight for the pantry to get himself a snack.

"Actually we've been looking at cars," Gammy said. "Karen showed us how to go to the various webs to compare prices and check for accident damage on used vehicles."

"Plus, the cardinal currently in charge of the Vatican taskforce forwarded money to Father Perez to distribute to the demon hunters in Oakfield since we're all legally dead and they can't pay us directly," Sister Joan added. "Latricia isn't the only one who needs a vehicle to get to work."

"Speaking of which, what time do you need to be at Java's Palace tomorrow, Gammy?" Wila removed her jacket and slung it over the back of the replacement chair for the one she accidentally cut in half and set on fire.

"You don't have to worry about me. Josie, the assistant manager, is going to pick me up on her way into work, and Penny will bring me home." Gammy smiled proudly.

Derek perched on one of the bar stools with his milk and cookies. Martin sniffed the plate and decided the over-processed treats weren't worth his attention.

"If you plan on sharing rides with Laura, make sure you buy something with room for your demon hunters." Wila grabbed a soda out of the refrigerator. "By the way, Crucifer is coming to the house tonight."

"You made a deal with a demon?" Sister Joan's English accent made her sound even more appalled than her words did.

"If it's a chance to stop Heaven and Hell's war and save the human race, we're taking it." Wila's phone vibrated in her pocket, and she pulled it out to check. Dani's text said she'd be here. Penny and Francine already responded while Wila had been waiting in the pick-up line.

"How are you going to entertain this demon if this place is warded against them?" Gammy demanded.

Wila looked at her angry grandmother and the flabbergasted nun. "He's not coming into the house. The Soccer Moms will talk to him on the patio while you two stay inside with Derek."

"Mom, you don't have to baby me," Derek protested with his mouth full of Oreos.

She glared at him. "Want to discuss Brittany kissing you some more?"

He turned back to the counter and started pulling homework from his backpack.

"Joan's right, baby girl," Gammy murmured. "I'm worried this demon will hurt you and your sisters."

Wila's gut clenched. "So am I, Gammy. So am I."

Chapter 24

"Bless you!" Wila said fervently when Penny handed her a large insulated reusable travel mug. Even with her winter coat on and a blanket over her legs, the weather guys weren't joking about tonight's temperatures dipping below freezing.

"I'm happy you're lazy and haven't stored your patio furniture for the winter yet," Penny responded as she passed out travel mugs to Francine and Dani.

The two women huddled together under another blanket on the wicker couch. Flames licked the small logs in the portable fire pit, but their heat barely made a dent against the incredibly still night air. Yep, a hard frost would definitely come tonight.

"How's Derek feel about not going to his dad's any time soon?" Penny asked as she settled on the other chair and wrapped the third blanket around herself.

"He's actually happy not to go." Wila sipped her white chocolate mocha before she added, "After the ex-louse saw Courtney's recording, he tried to pump our son for information about the Soccer Moms, me especially. Rashida playing the evil stepmother is not helping either."

"Speaking of Courtney, did I really see her climb out of your minivan this afternoon?" Francine asked.

Wila snickered. "Technically, that wasn't Courtney. That was Crucifer."

"Well, that explains the ass end of the demon I saw." Francine laughed.

"What is it with you and the potty mouth lately?" Dani stared at her seat mate. "Did the thousand demons you sent back to Hell short-circuit your verbal filter?"

"I guess I don't feel the need to put on a show anymore." Francine shrugged.

"You never had to put on a show with us," Penny protested.

"We all put on masks around other people." When Penny opened her mouth, Wila shook her head. "Every one of us does. You just ditched most of yours a lot earlier than the rest of us between the assholes you worked for and Justine getting sick. Francine lost hers in the battle with the demons at the high school. I'm trying to ditch mine because I don't want Derek to think I'm a bitter divorcée. As for Dani . . ."

"I know. I know." She slurped her double mocha. "I'm still playing the sweet little daughter who puts everyone else's needs before her own. I'm working on it."

"You could work on it while taking classes at UC-Oakfield," Penny muttered.

"Let's stop the Apocalypse first, then I'll enroll," Dani shot back.

Wila hid her smile behind her mug. Maybe there was hope for the shy, demure woman after all.

"Do I get any coffee?"

Wila knew who Crucifer would be wearing tonight, but hearing Pence's voice in her own backyard sent an electric shock through her. She looked over her shoulder. Pence, or rather Crucifer, walked towards the patio from the garage side of the house. He wore an Oakfield police uniform.

"I hope your neighbors don't mind, but I parked a couple of houses down the street." He jabbed a thumb in the general direction behind him.

"As long as you're not there during garbage pick-up tomorrow morning, you'll be fine," Wila forced herself to quip.

"I've got caramel macchiato, which is Pence's standard order, or there's raspberry white chocolate mocha, which is Chance Paxton's usual," Penny said.

"I'll take Chance's preferred beverage." He perched on the ottoman next to Wila. "I've grown fond of the flavor."

Penny handed Wila one of the extra mugs. She held it out to Crucifer, but she couldn't help the shudder that ran through her when she touched Pence's fingers.

"Hey," he said gently. "Remember I'm in the driver seat. Not the asshole cop. Me, the angel who made sure you kept your son this morning."

Is that how Crucifer still thought of himself? As an angel?

"I-I know," she forced out. "It's just—"

"I get it." He shook his head. "I can see everything he's said and done to you. He makes a lot of the demons I know look like pansy-assed amateurs when it comes to cruelty." He took a sip of his coffee. "Thank you, Pestilence."

"You're welcome," Penny murmured.

He sipped his coffee again before he continued. "You are right about Pence, Lasser, and Jackson conspiring against the four of you. Pence blames all of you for his grandmother's second death. Most of his friends have abandoned him after a confrontation between him and Lucas Manewell."

"You know Lucas?" Francine asked.

"Not personally." Crucifer shrugged. "I assign the incoming demons to keep tabs on any local taskforce recruits."

"You what?" Wila glared at the demon.

"I need them occupied, out of my hair, and away from you ladies if our plan is going to work," he said dryly.

"Pence, I understand," Penny said. "I don't get Deion and Courtney."

"It's all about power, my dear." Crucifer raised his cup. "Lasser is losing it within your little parents' association with your seduction of her second-in-command with free drinks and free food. Jackson replaced our darling War when he realized he couldn't control her. Now, he fears she has far more influence than he does, and he fears losing his son to her."

"Ohmigod," Dani murmured. "This is all so petty when we're facing the end of everything."

"What were you saying about my language a few minutes ago?" Francine said.

However, Wila didn't miss Crucifer's wince at Dani's mention of the Almighty. That meant he feared one being above the Devil.

"How do we keep them out of the way long enough for us to take out the Devil and broker a truce?" Penny said.

"There's more to it than keeping the trio out of our way," Crucifer said. "This kind of hatred in humans is what turns them into demons."

"Are you serious?" Wila blurted.

"Always when it comes to the Apocalypse," he replied.

"Are you telling us the truth when you say a human's extreme hatred is what turns them into demons?" Penny clarified.

He sighed. "I already swore an oath to you four I'd be truthful, factual, and not withhold information by omission. I cannot break that oath without certain repercussions. Unlike you human women," he added bitterly.

Wila had been doing her own reading of the Bible. She may not be the expert Francine and Penny were, but Wila remembered the passage that insinuated angels had babies with human women.

"What was her name and what did she do to you?"

Crucifer's startled expression was worth her question. His motivations started making sense.

"That's why you went along with Lucifer?" Wila continued. "So you could stay with your baby momma?"

Red that had nothing to do with the firelight flushed his cheeks and ears as he stared at the mug in his hands. "You wouldn't understand."

"Try us," Wila said softly.

"Azadeh didn't betray us. It was her sister."

"By us, do you mean you and Azadeh?"

He nodded. "Lucifer promised me she and our children would be safe. Her own sister sold her out to the priests who told Michael and the rest."

Wila swallowed hard. "The other side punished you for rebelling by killing them."

He nodded again and his head remained bowed.

"That's why you want us to help you take out Lucifer?" Penny blurted. "You blame him for failing?"

His head jerked up. "No! I just want this stupid war to stop. To answer your question clearly and plainly, Pestilence, yes, it is hatred held too long in a human's soul that destroys the soul and turns the human into a demon."

"Thank you," Wila murmured as she took Crucifer's hand. "Thank you for letting us understand."

The question now was how the hell were they going to make Pence, Courtney, and Deion understand the danger they were putting themselves in by traveling the path of hatred and vindictiveness.

Chapter 25

Wila needed to change the subject before she developed any more sympathy for Crucifer. "Do you actually have a plan for trapping Lucifer? Because I'm sure we are not traveling to Hell."

The demon shrugged. "I planned on telling him I captured the Four Horsemen and ask him if he wanted the enjoyment of killing them himself."

"Let me guess," Wila said dryly. "You'll put us in cuffs to sell the experience."

"I was thinking more like chains." He grinned.

Wila made a sour face. "I knew getting tied up would come in somewhere in your plan."

"No." Penny slashed the air with the blade of her hand. "First, it's too obvious. Second, I'm not going to be helpless in any encounter with him."

"Why not have Crucifer tell him we're meeting at Java's Palace after hours?" Wila shrugged. "He'll think he's catching us by surprise."

"That won't go over well with Karen," Francine said. "She'll demand we have backup."

"Then we do it without the demon hunters." Dani shook her head. "I don't want to be responsible for their lives in a battle with the Devil."

"Then the question is when," Francine murmured.

"I'm on shift tomorrow night," Wila said.

"Saturday night." Penny watched Crucifer. "Let's get this over with."

Once Crucifer left, Wila finally relaxed until Dani asked, "We're not really going to walk into an encounter with the Devil without backup, are we?"

"Hell, no!" Wila threw up her hands. "You know damn well he's going to bring an army of demons with him."

"We just need to keep them out of the sensing range of the demons until we need them," Francine said.

"That may be tough if Crucifer has his people watching our people," Wila pointed out.

"True." Francine nodded. "I'll discuss the situation with Karen tonight and get back to you." She hesitated a moment before she said, "Do we still want to set another appointment with Andy? I told him I'd call him tomorrow once we knew what our availability was."

"I think we should go through with it," Penny said.

Wila looked at Dani who shivered despite her coat, hat, and blanket. "I know it was my idea, but I won't push you if you're not comfortable with this."

She remained quiet for a long time, the cracks and pops of the burning wood the only sound. Even the traffic from Evans Road was muted.

Finally, she inhaled. "You're right, Wila. I need to get over myself. Hell, everybody in town is learning about us whether we like it or not."

Francine opened her mouth, but Dani held up her hand. "However, I think we need to give Mayor Oldham, Chief Wright, and all the Oakfield religious leaders a heads-up before we commit to an actual commercial."

Penny sighed. "She's right. Last thing we need is a backlash because of something we aren't thinking of. They all would be good sounding boards."

"I hate to say it, but we might want to talk to Coach Cordero again," Wila added. "He's the expert on too much publicity turning into a bad thing. While I get why he doesn't want to be involved in our plan, he might have some suggestions."

Friday morning, Wila drove straight to Deion's office after she dropped Derek off at school. The demon hunters arranged themselves around the building to keep an eye on all the entrances. With Father McAvoy still nursing a sprained knee, Karen had taken over day-to-day command of the Saint Michael's contingent, and she doubled the guards on the Soccer Moms' kids after Deion's custody suit.

Dani had called Coach Cordero and asked if he had any advice about the Soccer Moms' commercial idea. He didn't, but she followed up with why he didn't heal the priest's knee at the same time as he healed the damage from Father McAvoy's stroke. The coach said the Soccer Moms' may need the priest's experience, but he needed to learn not to compete with the younger and/or resurrected hunters.

The steering wheel resisted Wila when she tried to pull into a parking spot. The radio blared to life. "We should—do this—together."

"I understand you're trying to protect me, baby." Wila smiled. "But us charging in together is only going to make Deion more afraid. I know damn well you, Silver, Verde, and Sable were eavesdropping on our conversation with Crucifer last night."

"What is—war—good for?"

"Baby, I don't know what it's like for you in Heaven, but one of the hardest lessons for humans to master is knowing when to fight. This isn't the time or place."

"Fine—don't make me—say I—told you so," Scarlett grumbled.

"I won't make you, but we both know you'll do it anyway if Deion proves me wrong," Wila teased.

"Be—careful," Scarlett added as Wila opened the door and slid out of the minivan/horse. She almost sounded—scared.

"Always."

Wila charged across the parking lot and through the front doors of the building housing Reilly, Craig, and Sheffield. The bills for the receptionist's bribe were already between Wila's fingers as she approached the desk.

Deion had tried to get Sally fired for refusing to sleep with him, so Wila made sure she recompensed the woman the handful of times she'd made surprise visits to her ex-husband.

"Is he by himself in his office?"

Sally made a face and nodded. "As far as I know, but he's moved to one of the sixth floor corner offices. Left, right, end of the hall."

"Have lunch on me." Wila flashed her a bright grin as she slipped Sally the bills, and she headed for the elevators.

When the car doors opened on the sixth floor, Sally's directions led straight to his assistant Eileen stationed right outside Deion's door. She stood and raised her hands. "You can't go in there."

"Watch me." Wila walked right past her and opened the door to Deion's office. At least, he wasn't bumping uglies with another woman on his desk. He'd shed his jacket while he worked. She shut the door in Eileen's face and locked it. "We need to talk."

"Eileen will have the police up here any minute, so you'd better talk fast," he snapped.

"You were right. You are in danger."

He blinked at her admission. "Are you saying you still love me?"

"No, but your feelings about me can possibly turn you into a demon." She shook her head. "When we stop the Apocalypse, Derek will still need his father. I don't want him to lose you."

He smoothed his tie. "You have all the cards."

"And you've got Hannity working on an appeal as we speak. All I'm asking is that you drop the whole custody thing for now. I'll have Lilah, or probably Chance, petition the court so you can have Derek over Christmas vacation this year like you're supposed to, and I'll arrange to have guards for you all during that time period. But, Deion, if you and Rashida don't let go of your anger and hatred of me, it's going to turn you into something Derek won't recognize. Do you really want to do that to your own child?"

"How do I know you're telling the truth?"

"Talk to Reverend Sanford. If you don't believe him, I don't know how else to save you." She turned to leave.

"Wila?"

She looked over her shoulder.

"Is there anything between you and Paxton?"

She hesitated for a moment, the desire to lie in order to hurt Deion almost overwhelming. But like both Coach Cordero and Crucifer said, she had free will. If stopping the Apocalypse meant showing a little kindness to her ex-husband, she needed to be the bigger person. She turned to face Deion.

"No. We met Tuesday night when I chewed him a new one for leaning against my rig at the park. You heard what happened to Ms. King while we were in court yesterday. I had to eat a little crow when Lilah called him at the last minute to cover for her. Why do you ask?"

"I want to know if your generosity over Christmas is because of him."

She laughed. She couldn't help it. "I am not stupid enough to fool around with anyone while Gammy's living with me." But it reminded her of something she needed to discuss with Deion. "Have you talked to Derek about sex?"

Deion blinked slowly. "Excuse me?"

"He's started to show interest in girls." She paused, but Deion said nothing. "I've talked about the basics, but it would be better if the deeper stuff came from you as his dad."

"All right." Deion seemed to be taking her seriously.

Which was . . . weird as hell.

"And call him," she added. "Let him know things are okay between the two of you."

"I will."

For the first time ever, she felt like she was talking to the real Deion. She dared to shift her sight. The aquamarine crystal essence of her ex's soul was cracked as she feared, and gray stained the crack itself. But it wasn't too late for him.

Not yet.

She blinked.

"What did you just do?" he whispered hoarsely.

"I'm sorry, but with Derek's safety on the line, I had to know the truth."

"Wh-what truth?"

"Whether or not you are still human."

"D-did I see your soul?" He didn't seem to be angry by what she did. More awestruck than anything.

"Yes." She grimaced. "Unfortunately, it's a two-way street, which is why I rarely take a peek at anyone's soul. Is there anything else we need to talk about concerning Derek?"

Deion shook his head.

"All right. Later then." She pivoted, unlocked his door, and strode out of his office.

As he warned, two rent-a-cops jogged up the hallway towards Eileen's desk.

"Don't worry, guys." Wila imitated Francine's breezy wave. "I'm leaving."

One of the bozos tried to grab her arm. She sidestepped him and smiled while releasing a thread of her power. The stink of fear poured from him.

Actually, it came from his partner and Eileen, too.

"Didn't your mother ever tell you it's impolite to touch a lady without her permission?" Wila continued down the hallway.

The rent-a-cops didn't follow.

She reached the elevators and pressed the down button. Her reflection gazed back from the polished stainless steel doors. She actually looked pretty damn fine with red eyes.

Chapter 26

When Wila reached the station later that afternoon, she hunted down Jensen first thing to deliver his box of Long Johns and a fervent thank you for covering her shift yesterday.

He blushed and shrugged. "I needed the extra hours. We're still getting caught up on bills with Kerri having to take so much time off."

"Hey, if you ever need a baby sitter, give me a call."

He grinned. "I will."

She strode into the locker room and changed. Despite arriving at the station super early, Brian still managed to beat her to the rig. Somehow.

He paused in checking the supply lockers. "Should I ask why you had to take yesterday off?"

"Deion found out about Gammy living at my house." She tossed her uniform coat on the driver's seat. "And he found out the truth about me. His attorney scheduled an emergency custody hearing, and I wasn't sure how long I'd be at the courthouse."

Brian muttered an obscenity. "I'm sorry. Maggie didn't call me about the hearing until after nine yesterday. You should have called me. I would have gone with you. Please tell me the judge didn't go for his stupidity."

"First of all, I had plenty of backup with me. However, the stunt blew up in the ex-louse's face." She crossed her arms and leaned against the rig. "Judge Tellerson gave me full custody until the end of the Apocalypse."

"Did she actually put that in her order?"

"Her exact wording was 'until we all go to Heaven or the Soccer Moms of the Apocalypse stop the world from ending.'"

"Wait a minute." His eyes widened. "She knows?"

Wila debated how much truth was too much, but Brian had been at the soccer field on Tuesday. "Unfortunately, the truth is getting around despite the mayor's best efforts. Courtney Lasser's video notwithstanding."

Brian shook his head. "I may not be a lawyer, but that order is certainly not going to fly with an appeals court."

"Probably not, but it buys me a little time." Wila hesitated before she blurted, "Can I ask your honest opinion on something?"

"Shoot."

"What would you think if the Soccer Moms of the Apocalypse aired a TV commercial and revealed themselves to the public?"

"You said word is already getting around about you and your friends."

"But shouldn't we control the narrative instead of letting people make up their own stories?"

"You're asking someone who stayed in the closet for years in order not to lose his football scholarship." He slammed the rig's locker doors shut. "I'm not trying to lay a guilt trip on you, but how would you going public affect your kids?"

Wila sighed. "I hadn't thought about that. I've been working so hard to compartmentalize Soccer Mom stuff versus real mom stuff—" She smiled at him. "Thanks for the reality check."

"Any time." They fist-bumped.

Keeping people like Brian and her sisters in her life kept her from doing any insanely stupid shit.

Near the end of shift, fatigue dragged on Wila's limbs while she drove back to the station. Brian snored softly in the passenger seat. The entire rig carried the cloying odor of smoke from the fire in downtown.

The Croy Building was registered as a National Historic Landmark. Or it had been until the raging blaze gutted it over the last five hours.

Luckily, all of the businesses on the first floor were closed for the night. However, the apartments on the other three floors had all been occupied. She and Brian alone had made three runs to the hospital as the other firefighters rescued the tenants. So far, all the apartment residents were alive though two were in critical condition—an elderly man who already suffered from COPD and a mother who received severe burns and cuts when a window explode from the heat while she herded her children down the fire escape.

Wila pulled into their bay at the station. Not even the insanely white lights of the station cause Brian to stir.

She nudged him gently. "Hey, partner. We're home."

He jerked upright, his eyes wide until his surroundings registered.

However, she recognized his expression. He'd been dreaming about the war. "You okay?"

"I'm fine," he muttered. "The smell of smoke gets to me sometimes." He jumped out of the rig before she could say anything else. She didn't blame him. She'd done the whole nightmare and run thing to Deion more than once in the early years of their relationship.

Wila may not have been totally innocent in the matter of her divorce. She only wished Deion had talked to her, rather than nailing nearly every woman she knew.

She climbed out to find Kiera McDonald, the only other female paramedic in Oakfield, waiting for her. McDonald's freckled nose wrinkled at the odor that followed Wila.

"I heard about the five-alarm on the news." She shook her head. "You and Tucker go home. Fuller and I will restock the rig for you."

"I can't—" Wila started.

"It's Friday night." The younger woman smiled. "And isn't this your weekend with Derek?"

"Fuller's going to be pissed at you for volunteering him."

McDonald's smile turned into a full-fledged grin. "Aren't you the one who taught me not to let the guys get away with stuff by being nice?"

Wila chuckled.

"Besides, my only request is the same as Jensen's, but chocolate frosting only."

"You're on, but I'm not on duty again until Monday."

"I can wait."

Wila frowned. "What about Fuller? Isn't he allergic to chocolate?"

"He can negotiate his own damn payment," McDonald retorted.

Wila laughed all the way to the locker room. She didn't bother changing into her civvies. Without a shower, they'd reek as much as her uniform by the time she got home. She grabbed her bag and headed to the employee parking lot.

Her phone rang the instant she settled into Scarlett's driver seat. Wila glanced at the caller ID.

Courtney Lasser.

The only reason Wila could think of for the president of the parents' association to call would be for more harassment. On the other hand, Courtney may say something stupid enough Crucifer could use against her in court.

Wila tapped the answer icon, then the record function. "What do you want, Courtney?"

"Please help me," Courtney whispered. "Pence is at my house and he's threatening to kill me and Kenny because I didn't make sure you lost Derek at the hearing."

Crap. Had Crucifer's possession of the cop last night finally broken him for good?

"Where's Rick and Kimberly?"

"Rick took her to Madison to look at colleges. Please, Wila, I don't know what to do."

"Hang up. Call 9-1-1—"

"Who the fuck are you talking to, bitch?" Pence roared in the background. Then came the unmistakable sound of flesh striking flesh. A cry of pain. The line died.

Scarlett shifted underneath Wila until she was astride her horse.

Crucifer strode out of the shadows of the dumpsters. He possessed Chance Paxton again. "What's wrong?"

"You may have broken Pence. Scarlett?"

She neighed and tossed her mane.

"Come on." Wila held out her right hand and pulled him up onto Scarlett behind her. He wrapped his arms around her waist. She'd never admit it, but it was kind of nice to be held by him.

The horse raced past the station house while Wila called Penny. "Emergency at the Lasser house. Pence has gone off the deep end."

At least in her fatigues as War, Wila no longer smelled like the blaze at the Croy Building.

Chapter 27

Neither Penny nor Dani asked any questions of Wila when Silver and Verde caught up with Scarlett. Not even why Crucifer tagged along. The three horses raced toward the gated subdivision where both the Lassers and the Coy-Astins lived. Of course, it was well after midnight, and everything was locked up tight for the night.

That didn't stop the Mares of the Apocalypse from leaping lightly over the closed gates and galloping down the street. Francine and Sable waited for them four houses away from the Lassers' home. The downstairs lights glowed in their target, but the window blinds were closed tight.

"Anything?" Penny asked.

"I circled around the subdivision." Francine shook her head. "Neither Pence's truck or any Oakfield PD vehicle is within the walls. Sable and I even peeked in everyone's garages, except Courtney's. I didn't want to accidentally let them know we're out here."

"He could have climbed over the wall and walked in on foot," Dani ventured.

"Or his vehicle could be in the Lassers' garage," Wila said. "Courtney said Rick took Kimberly to Madison for a college weekend."

"It's not Pence inside with Courtney Lasser," Crucifer murmured. "It's Lucifer."

The blood in Wila's veins turned to ice. Were they remotely ready for this confrontation? "I'm not sensing any other demons."

"All the homes in the neighborhood are warded except for Courtney's,"

Crucifer said. "If he brought reinforcements, he's shielding them in her house. And he knows we're out here."

Wila eyed him over her shoulder. "Everyone?"

"Everyone."

"Ideas for getting inside and subduing Lucifer before he hurts Courtney and Kenny?" Penny asked.

"She's already suing me, and she slapped you," Wila said. "We could turn around and go home."

"Wila!" Francine stared at her like she'd grown a second head. Dani cackled.

"If you believed that, you wouldn't have come to her rescue," Crucifer murmured in her ear.

"If he already knows we're out here, let's just knock on the door," Dani rattled.

"I'm with you," Penny said. "Dani, you ring the doorbell like we did at Pence's house. The rest of us will jump in via our steeds with weapons blazing."

"I don't have a pair of flaming scales," Francine said sourly.

"You know what I meant." Penny nudged Silver around so they faced the others. "You and Sable grab Kenny and get him to your house for safety. Come back for Courtney."

"Because I'm the most useless Soccer Mom?" Francine bit out.

"No, because your house is the closest refuge," Wila snapped back. "You did tell Karen what's going on?"

Francine nodded. "She and Neal are watching the entrances at our house. Brittany took Rose down to the panic room."

"You guys aren't going in the back like we did at Pence's house?" Dani asked.

"Why bother?" Penny shrugged. "If Crucifer's right, and Lucifer knows who's out here and where we are, there's no advantage. Shall we, ladies and gentledemon?"

Everyone murmured their affirmatives.

Penny and Silver trotted toward the Lassers entryway. The rest of the horses followed suit. Silver stepped to the side to make way for Verde to approach the front door.

Dani jumped down from her horse. Wila always expected Dani's bony heels to make clicking sounds on concrete, but Death was quieter than a church mouse on Christmas Eve. She pressed the doorbell.

A shadow moved behind the fleur de lis half-window at the top of the door.

"Now," Penny hissed.

Scarlett gathered herself and leapt, but she stopped abruptly. Or something stopped her.

Wila and Crucifer flipped over the horse's head and crashed through the wall.

Chapter 28

Wila smacked the floor hard on her right shoulder despite Courtney's expensive carpeting. When Crucifer landed on top of Wila, she feared she had dislocated her sword arm.

More crunching and cracking plus a shriek of alarm from Penny said she and Francine had encountered the same issue. They may have powers as the Soccer Moms of the Apocalypse, but gravity still ruled the universe.

Crucifer scrambled off Wila. She rose to find Pence, or rather Lucifer, holding a semi-automatic handgun to Kenny's head. Tears trickled down the kid's face. She couldn't blame him for the very real fear he was feeling now. Meanwhile, Dani struggled to keep a sobbing Courtney from running to her son.

"Oh, Crucifer," the Devil mocked. "You are so going to pay for your betrayal."

Wila expected anger, or even hatred from the demon with her. Instead, a wash of sad weariness poured from him.

"You need to let your hatred go, brother."

"After what He did to us?" the Devil shouted.

"All you had to do was say you were sorry," Crucifer said. "You let your damn pride get in the way."

"He stooped too low when he made the Kid one of them!"

"So why aren't you going after the Kid instead of these worthless humans?" Crucifer asked.

The Devil hesitated for a second before his mouth split into a rictus that could barely be called a smile. "Oh, you poor idiot. You went and fell in love with one of your pets again."

He whipped the barrel from Kenny's temple and aimed at Wila so fast she saw the flash of the muzzle as he fired. Courtney screamed. Crucifer knocked Wila to the carpet, but all she could see was black smoke pouring from Chase Paxton's body. And all she could hear was the sound of wings.

She shoved Paxton's body off her. Penny pulled Wila to her feet while Francine grabbed the unconscious man and disappeared through one of the holes in Courtney's living room wall.

Wila's jaw dropped as the smoke coalesced into the most gorgeous hunk of manhood she'd ever seen. And that was without the black-feathered wings protruding from his back.

He half-leapt half-flew at the Devil, who was still inside Pence's body. The gun hit the floor and bounced once on the thick carpet before coming to a rest. By some miracle, it hadn't misfired.

Penny kicked the firearm under the couch and debris where the wall and windows used to be before she nocked an arrow in her bow.

Wila drew her sword. A quick glance showed Courtney, Kenny, and Dani were gone. Hopefully, Dani had gotten the other woman and her son clear of the house. The damage to the Lasser home was already worse than the demon battles in Penny's and Francine's places.

Unfortunately, Crucifer's wingspan blocked any clear shot at Pence.

"Disengage, Crucifer!" Wila screamed.

He glanced at her with coal black eyes before he delivered a right cross that should have taken off Pence's head.

"Yes, brother," the Devil purred. "Walk away while I entertain your pet."

His comments only infuriated Crucifer further. He tossed the Devil through one of the remaining slivers of the front living room wall before he folded his wings and dove through the adjoining hole.

Wila raced out of the house after them, Penny on her heels. In the yard, the two fallen angels traded blows. Dani and Francine had come back. Between the Soccer Moms and their steeds, the Devil was surrounded.

The women danced around the two combatants, but no one could manage a shot without accidentally killing their ally in the process. Neither the Devil or Crucifer bothered with English anymore. They sang in the angelic language. From the glass cracking in the second floor windows and the outdoor security fixtures exploding, whatever they sang wasn't very polite.

Lights flickered on in the surrounding homes at the strange noises coming from the Lassers' front yard. Wila prayed no one was stupid enough to come outside and lose the protection of their wards.

Spotting an opportunity, Wila aimed a thrust at the Devil's side. He swung Crucifer around by the neck to block the sword, and she narrowly avoided skewering him. But the move left the Devil's back wide open.

Penny launched an arrow at his exposed ribs.

Except, somehow, the Devil caught the arrow.

He whirled and plunged it into Crucifer's chest. The fallen angel exploded in a cloud of feathers.

Chapter 29

"No!" Wila screamed. She leapt at the Devil, swinging her sword at his neck.

He didn't move. He simply was no longer there.

The miss sent Wila sprawling on the dormant grass.

"No," she repeated over and over. She tried to grab feathers, but a wind sprung up. The plumage fluttered and whirled out of the yard and down the street to disappear into the night.

All except one pinion feather she clutched to her chest. Tears rolled down her face. This was worse than Afghanistan. She failed. Big time. There wasn't even a body to bury.

Francine walked over and knelt beside her. "I'm sorry, honey, but we need to leave. People are filming us again. Dani's doing her best to kill the videos, but she may take down the entire power grid if we don't get out of here."

Wila picked up her sword and sheathed it before she climbed to her feet. However, she didn't dare let go of the feather.

Wila remained slumped on one of Francine's brand-new kitchen chairs. She wasn't sure how much time had passed, but the mug of white chocolate mocha had grown cold in her left hand. Her right hand still clutched the feather against her heart. Her sisters returned after settling Courtney and Kenny at Helen Chow's house for the night. However, Wila had to force herself to interact with the other Soccer Moms through the numbness consuming her.

"What about Paxton?" she murmured after Penny finished her update.

"We took him home," Dani said. "His mom and two demon hunters are staying with him. We're not taking any more chances with demon victims."

"Honey, there's something you should know." Francine pulled her chair closer to Wila's and wrapped her arm around Wila's shoulders. "Chance's baby brother was a community activist in Chicago. He was killed in a gang shooting this summer. Their mom said Chance wasn't dealing with the loss very well. That's how he got possessed."

"Crucifer saw the same pain and loss in Chance he felt, but they were two different people." Wila looked up and met each woman's gaze.

"And it's probably why Crucifer approached you first," Dani said.

"You lost Heath—" Wila began.

"Through someone's stupidity. That drunk driver didn't intend to kill my husband. But the assholes who shot your mom and brother, the one who shot Chance's brother, heck even the angels on Heaven's side, they all did what they did intentionally."

"But we not only lost our one ally in Hell, we failed to take out Lucifer when we had the chance." Her failure ate her alive, but she couldn't escape it, much less stop it.

"He's not going away," Penny said grimly. "But maybe we need to reconsider our options. Come at this problem from an angle that doesn't include sneak attacks and battles in our houses and yards."

"Maybe—" Dani cocked her head and stared at Wila. "Did you do something to Crucifer's feather?"

"No." Wila looked down, half-expecting the pinion to be disintegrating, like the ash Francine had encountered with the demons' smoke forms.

Instead of black, the vanes, shaft, everything was white.

She swallowed hard. "Why did it change color?"

"Because he sacrificed himself to save you," Francine murmured. "And he was forgiven."

Chapter 30

Saturday night, Wila wrapped herself in her coat and blanket before she curled up on the wicker couch on her patio. A few stars penetrated Oakfield's light pollution to glitter against the black velvet sky. The weather report suggested they might have flurries on Wednesday.

The numbness of the last twenty-four hours was starting to wear off, and pain settled in her bones. Maybe that was why she came out here after dinner. Regain some of that numbness. It had served her well after Mom and Watende's deaths.

The back door squeaked. Gammy came outside, bundled in a coat and a blanket like Wila. Gammy closed the door before she waddled over to the couch and sat beside Wila.

"You punishing yourself?" Gammy asked.

"No." Wila shook her head. "I've killed plenty of demons to save people. It's stupid to get upset over this one."

"He knew what he was getting into by taking on the Devil, baby girl." Gammy patted Wila's thigh. "In the end, he made the choice to stop acting like a demon. You were a good influence on him."

"Why do you say that?"

"Baby girl, I maybe dead and risen, but how a man looks at a woman he's in love with doesn't change."

"That's ridiculous," Wila retorted. "He wasn't capable of those feelings."

"Weren't you and your sisters the ones who said he sided with Lucifer because the angels planned to murder his wife and children?"

"Yes."

"My guess is you reminded him of his wife." Gammy chuckled. "And you, my dear baby girl, have always had a thing for bad boys."

Wila glared at her "Is that why you never told me about Deion's other baby mamas?"

"Would you have believed me if I had?"

Wila's mouth opened, but no words came out. She hadn't tolerated anybody telling her anything when she was a teenager. And she pulled the same kind of crap when she had been honorably discharged.

"I'm sorry for acting the fool, Gammy." She leaned her head against Gammy's shoulder.

"Instead of freezing our butts out here, why don't we take a spin in my new car and get some cinnamon buns for breakfast in the morning?"

Wila straightened. "For breakfast?"

"All right. Two packs of buns. One for tonight and one for tomorrow."

"But that's wasting money, Gammy," Wila teased.

Gammy stood. "Baby girl, life is too damn short not to live it fully."

"Is that why you and Laura picked out the same make and model as Karen's sports car?"

"It's got plenty of trunk room for holy water," Gammy said haughtily.

"Not to mention you can pick up guys in it."

"You hush up, baby girl." But there was a definite gleam in Gammy's eyes.

Wila laughed and followed Gammy back into the house. Maybe they should pick up more cinnamon buns for next week's girls' night.

They gathered Sister Joan and Derek. When the quartet passed through the family room on their way to the garage, the white feather rocked in its place next to Grandpapa's clock on the mantel.

Wila smiled. She hoped Crucifer was reunited, somewhere, with his own family.

With the Devil loose in Oakfield, the Soccer Moms of the Apocalypse need to find a way to stop him from igniting the final war. But how? Especially when Dani considers forgoing her duties as Death in order to keep her resurrected husband.

Turn the page for a thrilling sneak peak of
Death in Double Mocha!

Death in Double Mocha

Irritated as hell, Dani Elante jabbed the button to open her garage door. Mark had forgotten to haul the garbage can out to the curb for tomorrow morning's trash pick-up.

Again.

Her normally conscientious son seemed to have totally lost his mind with the onset of puberty. He had barely acknowledged her presence when she marched into his bedroom and lectured him, his earbuds jammed in his ear canals and his nose firmly affixed to his phone screen as his thumbs typed messages to his friends. If her brother Marty hadn't put her and Mark on his family's unlimited phone plan, she would have had to take a second mortgage out on the house to pay for her son's excessive usage.

She should have grounded Mark, but guilt nagged her. He pretended to be okay with her being the avatar of Death, one of the Four Horsemen of the Apocalypse.

Or rather the Soccer Moms of the Apocalypse, as Wila had coined them.

But the four women's kids only had each other to talk to when it came to the weirdness of what was going on in Oakfield over the past couple of months. Deep down, she knew she couldn't take those relationships away from Mark. It was his only outlet for dealing with the madness.

A cold wind rattled the tree branches and the handfuls of dried brown leaves clinging to them in the dark. The dang bitter breeze also cut through her sweatshirt and jeans and raised goosebumps along her skin. She should have grabbed her coat before she came out.

The scent of smoke blew along the freezing air along with the hint of the coming winter to Illinois. Someone in the neighborhood was fighting the late fall chill with a cozy wood fire.

A sense of regret whispered through her. Maybe she shouldn't have sold the old Victorian she and Heath had started to refurbish before his accident. She loved the odor of pine and the crackle of real wood burning while cuddling with her husband in front of the flickering flames. But there was no way to pay two mortgages on just her salary, and Mark needed consistency with the loss of his father.

Dammit, Heath had been gone for six years. She was not going to wind herself into another depressive funk. Just because nearly everyone else she knew had family members rise from their graves, it didn't mean she'd get that lucky. Except the question was almost as nagging as her guilt. Had Heath not been righteous enough to deserve resurrection with the Second Coming of Christ?

Or was he still in his grave because she was Death?

Dani grabbed the handle of the garbage can and dragged it out to the curb before she went back for the recyclables container. She wheeled the blue recyclables can out to the curb and set it beside the pink trash can that promoted breast cancer awareness. Why did she miss Heath so much when she barely thought about Mom?

The better question is why hadn't either of them risen when half of the Oakfield Cemetery's residents had come back to back life a few days before Halloween. They were both good people. Why did Penny get her mother-in-law and Wila get her grandmother back, and Danielle was still alone? It wasn't fair.

But then, it wasn't fair she had been chosen as Death, one of the Horsemen of the Apocalypse either.

A gust slapped her ponytail in her face. It was too damn cold to bemoan her luck in life outside. She'd make a hot cup of green tea and pout under her favorite blanket. Nope, she'd binge her favorite sitcom until she fell asleep. Marty would understand as both her brother and her boss when she called in sick in the morning. She turned to head back into the garage.

The oak tree in her front yard moaned, and a shiver ran down her spine that had nothing to do with the frigid wind. It was the same sensation of wrongness she felt around one of the newly risen dead. She whirled around, looking for the cause, wishing for the first time the city of Oakfield had installed more streetlamps in their subdivision.

A dark figure stepped out of the shadow of the fence-lined right-of-way running between the Cassadines' and the Jones's houses across the street. She was on the verge of summoning her scythe when the shape shuffled into the square of the light cast by the fixtures in her garage onto the asphalt pavement. The blonde hair was as dirty as the clothes and face, but the piercing blue eyes were the same as the first time she met him.

Her heart threatened to choke her. "Heath?"

"Hey, baby." He looked terribly confused. "I think I had an accident."

Acknowledgements

Unlimited thanks go to Elaina Lee and JW Manus. I couldn't do what I do without these brilliant ladies.

More thanks go to the backers of the Soccer Moms of the Apocalypse. This book wouldn't have seen the light of day this year without your support and generosity.

A special thanks goes to MJ Silversmith who asked for a demon named Crucifer as part of her Kickstarter reward package. I immediately heard the Soccer Moms in the back of my head, making cruciferous vegetable jokes. Little did I know he'd turn into this book's anti-hero.

Much love goes to the Darling Husband and Bella, the Princess Pup for keeping me sane during the writing process.

And most of all, lots and lots of gratitude to the numerous first responders, not just our family members, who jump into danger to help those who need it.

SUZAN HARDEN transitioned from writing information technology manuals for companies and legal articles for a law enforcement magazine to her first love, fantasy and science fiction in all their forms. She's the author of the Bloodlines, the 888-555-HERO, and the Justice series.